IN THE FLESH

IN THE FLESH

A NOVEL

■

Ane Schmidt

translated by Anne Born

LONDON NEW YORK SYDNEY TORONTO

The right of Ane Schmidt to be identified as author of this work
has been asserted by her in accordance with the Copyright, Designs
and Patents Act 1988.

First published in Denmark in two separate volumes under the titles
Jeg and *Ham* by Gyldendalske Boghandel-Nordisk Forlag,
Copenhagen.
First published in one volume under the title *Anelser* by
Tiderne Skifter Forlag, Copenhagen.

This translation first published 1995 by Souvenir Press Ltd.,
43 Great Russell Street, London WC1B 3PA
and simultaneously in Canada

This edition published 1995 by arrangement with Souvenir Press Ltd

CN 1658

Published with a translation grant from the Danish Literature
Information Center

Phototypeset by Intype, London
Printed in Great Britain by
Mackays of Chatham plc, Chatham, Kent

i

I have taken to living like a nail, washed perfectly clean. I look at my body in the morning and I . . . I . . . In the past I had to get up and in and investigate, now I am ready. I am clean. I dry myself on my big white terry towel and lie myself down in my bed. It is air-tight, shut in all the way round. Now it's rising up, and I take my pills. We put on speed when the space ship sails through the night and suddenly opens its wings, I fall out and it runs through the body, the universe, like a little burning dot. I lie with my head pressed back. I open my mouth and the prick comes in, big and swollen, I suck and get wet. It goes on for hours. Cotton. White tape round my legs. Up to the knees. Around the thighs. And my cunt like a throbbing, bloodred fist.

I call it the new life. When I'm standing in the queue in the supermarket with my cheque book ready. I write one for 300, show my card, and both I and the cashier smile. Here she sits in her pink overall, I manage to think just before I fall out slantwise into the traffic. I will allow myself anything and everything, my life is so short. I whisper to myself. I want to be honest, pure. I have lived in Italy where the scooters grow. I have lived in Copenhagen, in the light. Now I shall live here. I just want to be, and live. Exist. If only I could forget that I am.

I get up. I sit in my room and look out over the rooftops, the walls. And know the cars drive along down below, and people walk in and out among each other, with handbags and newspapers. Cigarettes in their mouths and that English look when they talk to each other. I can sit like this and know everything. I've got things as I want them. I have sleep, the fridge, and this square white room as my lion's cage to pace around. That's all. The next time I'm born I will be the same. The same disappearing patch on the wall in the sun.

It's Sunday, and I sit here thinking. I can remember the white flowers I got as a child. And my father's face when I hurt myself and cried. He came close and leaned down over me. I loved him. We lived in a rented villa. I couldn't understand the language, of course, but I just invented my own. I lay in the garden. I sat and dreamed. Then I grew up and became inferior. I remember it all.

I am at a party. You could safely call it a party. It's my father's birthday. There's champagne even for breakfast and my father is in newly ironed pyjamas. His face is flat and oval, like a relief, tanned in the sun. I look across at him and he looks at me. I am wearing my best spotted dress, I look like a girl going to a dance, maybe I've fallen for a boy in my class. My father, my father. People come to the door the whole time, with presents. They laugh and talk. I look at my father as he goes from guest to guest pouring out drinks, handing round cigarettes and biscuits.

When I sit in front of the television I can see myself in the window, wide open to the warm evening. As I sit now I can see half my face, cut through vertically. One ear, one eye, half the nose, half the mouth. The forehead, cheek, hair. The neck, one shoulder, one arm. That's what is left of me.

I think. Now I stop thinking. From the open half of my brain white photographs rise into the air, from what I am watching on television, and the wall and the whole room. And the window. I am 33 years old. Half dead, half alive. The live part lies behind. The dead part on all sides. And something is in sight, something I want to walk into, like a child in a ski suit holding a biscuit, with a cloud of breath in the cold in front of its mouth.

I am in Rome. With my class. And in the night I creep into the teacher's room. I'll never forget it.

We all smoke. And we sit in the Piazza Navona like the other tourists. There's nothing to tell before night comes and bedtime. It's our second night in Rome.

There's the heat, the shutters and the rooms. We're in double rooms. Except the teachers, who have single rooms. It's our maths teacher. I'll never forget him. He's not young, not old. His randy kisses when he wakes and I'm sitting on top of him, and he's forgotten the situation, or takes it to be a dream, or how he makes it impossible to go on living without me and my body. My breasts, that he grabs

at in the dark, and my thighs, that I've placed on each side
of him, above his sex that's uncovered and grows until it
stands up and without hesitation slides in, almost pumps
itself up into me while his body lies quite still, only his
hands are up in my hair, he can't resist it.

He whispers: 'Don't ever tell anyone.' And comes, for
the first time, up in my cunt, straight away. I don't say a
word but wait for a little while, stroking his chest and
stomach, up and down, down his thighs, just being his,
now and here for a moment and then at once forgotten.
We both know it. He doesn't need to whisper. He's quite
safe, but he's frightened and sweats, but doesn't send me
away.

His nipples aren't big. Mine aren't specially big, but
much bigger than his. I have breasts. And I have my cunt,
which I want to use. I've tried schoolmates, but I want a
grown-up one. A real prick.

He's quick, I must say. But I wait for more. And it comes.
It stands up again, and he's got me lying down. We kiss.
He has hairy legs, and I am a little girl. His tongue deep
in my mouth, and vice versa, alternately, in a completely
open production of spit and muscle, it's almost too much.
It goes down my body, and I sweat. He turns me round,
on my knees, and I take it from behind, with my back
arched, arse up, in general acceptance. I am not experienced, but follow my own commands. His hand. First
round the hanging breasts, then round my stomach, and
up in the hairs, it finds the clitoris and the lips, open to
the prick's movements, and full of blood.

His breath on my neck, I remember it all. And I come. I
haven't tried it before, with a prick. It's the first time,
and then from behind with fingers and magnitude, with a
sudden dragging, swimming up and away. He comes as

well, the second time, and can't keep quiet but groans. I have never heard anything like it.

We lie side by side. I begin again. Move my hand down to his stomach and his prick, make it grow hard. I lie on my back, and he drives it in, now it knows the cunt. It is tender and warm and wet. I can keep on.

I sit and look at my brother who is masturbating. I can't be bothered to go to school, it's as simple as that. We read *Fanny Hill* all the time, go swimming and think of nothing but our bodies. I haven't yet discovered women's literature, and I don't have a speculum up my crotch. I fall into a reverie at the sight of my brother's prick.

I should like to understand the world. I decide to write everything down but forget about it next day. It's weird how I believe in aesthetics. I can pore over a piece of cartridge paper, and only write in black.

One day my mother comes out of the kitchen. She wears an apron and looks like a French lady. Then suddenly flies start buzzing around her, and she hits me right in the face. I don't know what comes over me. I scream, and get hold of her hair and push her and hit out at her. And she starts to weep. She sits down on a chair and raves about how awful I am. I know she'll get up soon and kiss me and say sorry, sorry, I didn't mean it.

I think: I'll sock her one as soon as she stops squawking.

I lie glaring at the wall for days on end. My father worries. What's the matter with that girl? But he doesn't say anything. I can lie quite still. I don't go down for meals, I get thinner and thinner. One morning I've disappeared into the sheets.

First the doorbell rings. Then it's the telephone. The bells shrill, but we don't care. It's my brother Poul who's in bed with me upstairs. We've been here all the morning on the point of it, and now we don't give a shit for the outside world. He's so beautiful. He's as brown as a little child, and I knew we'd be able to. So gentle, so soft. There's no hurry. He lies with his tongue on my right nipple. Then the left one. Then the right. They stand up, erect and hard, and he moves his tongue around them. I've got hands everywhere. On his buttocks, that are white to the edge of his trousers. On his back. Up to his neck. He wants to make me happy so much, and I tremble all over. We help each other. He licks me till I come. Then I take his prick and guide it in. This won't be the last time, I think, it won't be the last time.

I often think of Poul now he's an adult. What does he think about me? Does he remember the afternoons in our parents' house, and does he ever long for the garden and the cherries?

In Italy we always rode scooters. And not only that, we stood beside the scooters for hours on the square. Then we talked about nothing. My life has been lived in vain. I have never had any experience. But I have lived and lived, seen flowers, felt speed. There's nothing else. That's everything. It's beautiful. It's life.

One day we're on the scooter. Lizards whistle past.

I think of death. What will happen to my breasts? They will rot like apples in the earth, I can't live with it.

I have to admit I'm drunk. It's been a slow process. That's best. If only it works and my face spreads like pictures. There are boys everywhere. And suddenly there's one who falls in love with me. I wear clogs and jeans. He keeps on asking me questions about films I haven't seen. That doesn't matter. My writing is almost like script, rather large, and indifferent. I write postcards home but I'm not away. Then he asks me to go home with him. I say yes. Why not?

I've changed over to Kent cigarettes. Just because of the white filter. I can't bear cork-coloured filters on cigarettes. I tell him all this as we lie on his mattress and he goes to get a mineral water after we've fucked. He's full of energy, talks and talks. He stands there with his little willy and an expression of total happiness. He sits in the chair by the window gesticulating. I would like to be in love with him.

I am taking an exam in Danish. I can't concentrate. There's an orange on the table in front of me and a glass of water. When shall I eat the orange? Shall I start with that or wait till I can't remember. Words are flowing. The orange as cunt. I peel it and open it with its rude boats, put it in front of me on the brown table top with the papers. Shall I write notes or start the essay at once? What shall I write about? I can only think of the orange. I sit and get wet between my legs. I can't sit here and wank. I must ask permission to, I can't manage it, if there's a teacher standing outside the door listening.

After a few hours I've finished. I wrote about Stockhausen. The subject was 'A Composer.' I ride my bike through the suburbs, relieved and free. I think of the orange. Of cunt lips. The saddle I ride on. It's summertime, there are flowers. I am high.

Suddenly the bike unfolds long thin wings in the transparent air. I ride above the asphalt, above gardens and trees. I sail on a cloud with the saddle pressed up between my legs. I cycle and cycle. I rub my thighs against the leather and bend back my neck in my birth. I hear Stockhausen. I think: I shall have it off with Stockhausen on a deserted milky way. And electronic instruments whirl past. A mellotron can do everything. It can settle itself round the clitoris like foam rubber and lick with the violins and bang on the perineum with the drums. I am close to fainting. Everything's going round. I feel my youth clamped in my groin.

When I get home I squeeze an orange into a glass. The little red drops gather, and I let the juice run down the lips like pearls of blood. I have locked the door and sit with legs apart on my Kevi chair. I push the chair forwards with my toes until my cunt stands out and my knees point as far back as they can. The muscles on the inside of my thighs stretch, and I put my hand slowly down and dip my fingers into the hole. The clitoris in its little hiding place, like an eye standing out. A pupil that looks straight into the mirror and sends out its threads like a jellyfish on the beach. I throw out my chest and my stomach muscles contract so I have to bend down over the centre of a circle that finally gives.

It's summertime. I walk around the rooms naked thinking what it will be like when I grow up. I shall never work in a factory. I shall never work in an office. They'll never make me.

'The Rolling Stones, complesso musicale inglese: Mick Jagger (1944–), Brian Jones (1944–69), Keith Richard (1944–) Mick Taylor (1941–), Charlie Watts (1941–), Bill Wyman (1941–).' I'm reading *Enciclopedia Garzanti Universale*, 20ª edizione. My brain stands open. A butterfly flies in, or out. I'm tired, but have no plans to go to bed. 'Hey! Mr. Tambourine Man, play a song for me.' **Dylan**, Bob (1941–), cantante di musica folk statunitense.' I want to dream. What shall I dream about? '**narciso**, (Narcissus, fam. Amarillidacee) genere di piante bulbose con foglie lineari e fiori a corolla tubolare.' I want to dream. What shall I dream about? '**Narciso**, (mit). giovane bellissimo, mori per il vano amore della propria immagine riflessa in una fonte. Fu mutato dagli dei nel fiore omonimo.'

Postcards are sent from all round the world. So many love letters, so many messages. I collect love letters in a shoe box. I imagine a pair with high heels, but I wear espadrilles myself. Every sentence must stand straight in the mouth, my mother taught me that when I was small. I have a notice board I hang kissing words on from chocolate kisses. Stardust, blue on silver. The sweet lump in the mouth, like a tongue kiss. And the little motto, that gets hung up. I can sit and suck. My mother. Chocolate. Prick. Then my body goes soft, and heat runs up my spine. There's a small army of prickling microbes that gather at the loins and send their benign missiles into the skin.

I set my mind on growing older, but I can't. It doesn't matter how much literature I read. I have read the nouveau roman and *The Female Eunuch* too. I just can't take it seriously, that way. I can see the art in it all right, but I fall asleep. Then I go out to the fridge and make some iced water. Then I sit down and drink it. And when I have drunk it I can go on with the literary life for a while.

I shall grow old one day, I'm sure. If only I don't get laced up.

If I have a son I will send him a postcard. If I have a daughter I will send her a letter. A long letter about chocolates and willies. But just before I send it off I shall put it in a bowl and put a match to it. So she'll be free from it.

I lived in a commune and I couldn't cope with it. Everyone wanted to go to bed with me. Both before and after dinner, and before and after the discussions in the common room.

Jan in particular was eager. He was at university and knew everything about linguistics. He talked about the function of language the whole time, except when he was fucking. Then he just fucked. I had started to paint and would stand for hours in front of huge canvases. Then he came in and slipped his hand around my buttocks. I had a mattress on the floor and we lay down straight away.

Sometimes I couldn't stand it. I felt there should be some foreplay. Something to warm you up. So I moved out.

Now I live here, quite alone, and Jan comes to visit me as often as he feels like it.

I'm a little girl of 17. I wash my hair in henna. And write letters in big yellow envelopes. I have started reading Tao writings on All and Nothing and butterflies. I love saying Chuang Tzu and Lao Tzu. I meet my first girl friend, and I'm sure I am lesbian. Everything I do I do by printed matter. I'm on my toes the whole time and I want to be an artist. I want to paint and write and sing and dance. I go for long bike rides with my sweetheart. Her name is Alphonsina. And we can lie and tickle each other's stomachs with grass. Raymond Radiguet: *The devil in the body*, we read ten pages each and nearly die. '**Radiguet**, Raymond (1903–23), narratore francese. Il suo romanzo *Il diavolo in corpo* ha per tema le inquiete passioni di due giovani amanti.'

She has plaits, and my hair hangs loose to the shoulders. Her hair is black, mine is coloured. She looks at me, I look at her. We get hot for nothing, and lie for hours under water. We cool our skin with each other, we heat up our skin with each other. We slide out of each other, into each other. We lick like gliding snails, damp brocade, we are inside each other at the same time, with tongues sucked in by the red cunt of each.

Or on top of each other with nipples touching. Like flowers coiling in the wind, and pubic hair curling around each other's tuft, dark and fair, it is endless, and only beauty, only peace and waves, embrace, bonk.

One day we go into town, wearing dresses, arms round waists. It is the great moment when we kiss in the restaurant. First gently, on the cheek and the lips. Then hotly, long, tongues melting together like ardent guppies. We have demonstrated our love. It's noticed by people around us, drooping tits and their dried-up husbands.

And we go out into the night, entwined, and buy ice creams, sit down to drink wine, right under the noses of the old wankers, who'd jump at the chance of getting us back to their pads, but won't get it even if they begged and prayed, came creeping up with banknotes and big cars. We have each other and that's what we want. Can't you understand that?

I dreamed I was in bed with myself. I was a man with dark glasses and rough, sunburned hands. I had come down from the mountains that day and was unshaven, enough to be scratchy and not a beard. And I thrust into myself. I lay with legs apart and sighed and groaned, and I thrust my prick down hard. I came simultaneously in a long, screaming orgasm that went on and on.

I sat in a green armchair and my body jerked so I woke up. I looked down at my breasts, they were still there. Thank God. And I felt between my legs with a swift hand. It was wet, and there was no prick and big mountainous balls, but the most delicate cunt with waving palms and throbbing blood.

I'm at school for so many years that it must be enough for several pupils. When I study Latin I think of holidays with beer and schnapps and my father in a white summer hat. When I am being heard, I don't know what to answer. I am empty of words. I have everything else possible, briefs, a bikini at home, brown legs, a brother called Poul, a summery mood, a dream of an omelette with chives, a father, a mother, healthy interests, a store of TV news in my brain, and a hopscotch stone from my childhood when I played hopscotch on the road in front of the house and in the playground in every break. But the fourth declension, I don't know what that means. Is it something rude? Case. What's that? Ablative. Means nothing to me. It's a closed country.

Thøger Larsen. We read a poem by Thøger Larsen. It's good, I can remember it being good. It is very long, a man lies dying. All his life.

And then of course there are the school gardens. Legs up among the rhubarb leaves and long, red, juicy, tense stalks bursting with longing and flesh.

Otherwise nothing.

My back is sore from bonking. Day after day the same thing. I read about needles through nipples. Stand looking at the rubber pricks in the shops in town. A double dildo for two girls. I imagine myself sitting on one and clinging to Alphonsina, who sits on the other one. Why, actually? When we can lick the soft edges of each other's cunt till our tongues bleed, and slake our thirst in juice. But why not? Why not have the double prick in each of our holes and rub the hairs together, so the pubic bones clap together and the clitoris rubs and grows and vanishes for a moment in black stars. Why not?

I can't recall what I did when I was a child. But I could stand for hours looking at nothing. If only restlessness hadn't come plopping through the letterbox. If only my

body didn't shout and scream the whole time. Or what? If
I just had small doses of whipping from a loving hand that
could give my labia a bit of a flip to leave my clitoris free.

I lie reading about responsibility and punishment. About
guilt. Expiation. And about the State as law and order. I
hurry inside and shove my little battery-driven vibrator
up my arse.

Alphonsina far far away over mountains and passes. Me
with my school bag and a rainy day in its endless extent.
A dog barks. There's someone on the stairs. The door
opens. Inside the box is another box, exactly like the first
one.

I get undressed and dressed endlessly. It has all become so
mechanical with my age. I wash myself the whole time. It
is so hot that I only have to walk round the room once or
twice to be soaking wet with sweat. And have to change
my T-shirt. Every day I put on clean underpants. And
perhaps a couple of times during the day. And always if
I'm going out. I am not hysterical, but I would die of heat
if I didn't take a shower at least three or four times a day.

A man sits looking at me. He's sweating. He moves his
damp hand up my thighs. I can't stand it. I scream. He
gets hold of me and throws me down on a big bed, a
couple of mattresses tied together with twine. I pass out,
don't know what happens.

When I come into the world I'm lying in salt water.
There's a blue sky, big green palms, and a red moon. I am
quite naked and swim like a fish. I stay in the water, roll
on to my back and look up at the illuminated town.

When I get started on any stuff, I keep on. I haven't got

an inbuilt stop-light. Everyone drinks, obviously, but I stay with the stuff.

One Martini, one glass of wine, and there are smiles from all corners of the garden. I have two possibilities, either to go on or to drink water out of a beautifully cut glass, and smile just as much as the others.

There they are straight away with their moral censure. I don't give a shit, but it prolongs the morning after, their gaze, you know something's wrong.

I drink wine, what I can get at the table. Then I drink cognac. Yes, please, I say, looking innocent. Then I have to get to the bar, if there is one. Or in town, or in the cellar, or the attic. Nothing can stop me.

I'm drinking with a man from the insurance section, and I can see my father somewhere out of the corner of my eye. I can't stop. I take the bottle and go behind a bush. I've got my stiffener.

He goes on and on. I listen. Now I couldn't care less. I nod and think of more. More booze. I seize the chance to get hold of a bottle. I don't hold back. I come back smiling. Now he wants to go to bed with me, I can see.

'Sorry,' I say, 'I never fuck when I'm drunk.' (Which is a lie, by the way, I love fucking.)

'Oh,' he says, looking round quickly to see if anyone has heard what I said.

I sit with my breasts jutting out, in my low-cut dress, bent over my glass. Now it's a question of getting it filled as many times as possible. He talks on, and suddenly takes fright. He's thinking of my father.

Then I'm alone. It's my own problem. Nobody gives a hand. They are deep in conversations, luckily. And I fill up the glass, right to the brim. I settle down to enjoy the view while I lift it to my mouth, and down the stuff. Nothing can surprise me any more.

They say Scott Fitzgerald drank gin. I am with him on his white odyssey. 'Fitzgerald, Francis Scott Key (1896–1940), narratore statunitense, tipico esponente della società del dopoguerra; raggiunto giovanissimo il successo, ebbe poi una vita travagliata e mori quasi dimenticato a Hollywood. *Di qua dal Paradiso, Il grande Gatsby, Tenera è la notte.'*

In the morning I am fit again. I refuse to live my life in a hangover, no matter how ill I am.

Then I start again, if I can get at it. Unless I am free, and live without it for long periods, laughing and light. That's what I say, if I'm asked.

Alphonsina takes off her clothes. I'm roused to the tips of my fingers. I can't stay in the room. I have to go out.

Then I go in, naked too as she is, and shuddering with desire. There is a mirror between us. We see each other as transferred movements. But we are equally good at it.

The clitoris with its little rod. We don't have a prick hanging between our legs.

Then she turns round, and I see her shoulder and back. Her buttocks in the light. I go and stand vertically against her, and we stand in the air like sunlight, or like needles of hydrogen.

She whispers; I can't hear what she says. I say: 'What did you say?' And she whispers: 'Open up with your juice.'

I imagine Alphonsina is Poul's sister. And that I have insinuated myself into a sacred alliance. That I'm walking forbidden paths with my love.

The prick is crooked. There are no straight pricks. It stands in its own independent bow. It's absurd. If I was a prick manufacturer I would make a straight prick and serve it up with briefs-music.

His scrotum is working. I sit looking at my sleeping

Poul. It is a painting that has built in a little motor under the prick, which measures the temperature, or whatever it does. It is its own animal, with its own life, in its own zoological garden. I am the spectator. I walk around holding a balloon, I am a little girl on a wooden scooter. I have a mouth full of desire.

It can manage by itself. Without anyone rubbing it, it produces a drop, in foreplay. It slides up the duct and flattens itself on the glans, which is distended and coloured. I close my lips around it and suck with a good wet tongue.

I shall write a book. 'The Wanderings of the Prick' will be the title. 'Dedicated to my brother in grateful recollection of a hot summer.'

Brimstone butterfly. The lizard that falls down from the crumbling wall. Jolifanto bambla. I want to join in. Hi, Hugo Ball, I'm your woman tonight. I tread water. I've no strength left. I have been down for the first time. I have been down the second time. Hugo Ball, take me up into the golden age.

Bank chiefs knew nothing about pingpong over millions. 35 drowned in six weeks. Emergency meeting of the EC on the steel dispute. Supervisors look at Provincial Bank's 44 per cent interest rate. He learns to be a Dane during his holidays. Camre hits out at SF. Bank stormed after threat of bankruptcy. Many old people fainting. 62–year-old killed in parachute jump. New air strike on Beirut. IBM in Magasin's store. Peace People refuse to lead. Captain acquitted after wreck. Dames at the centre of Paris fashion. Record rainfall at swimming-DM. Bath water.

I'm fantasising, as usual. I would like to know how other

people's brains function. Can they toe the line? Don't they go round in circles? You can't identify with another person, with their intelligence. That doesn't have any skin or organs.

I sit in my place and let my fantasy loose. I give it a long rope, far out of the window, up above the asphalt and on. I write little notes, only about sex. I use the words for what they mean. And I send the notes around the class. We are in a maths lesson. I hope they end their journey on the teacher's desk. Anonymous and burning with youth.

One day I'll creep inside the teacher. In under his skin. Up into his body. I will suck him awake with my spit, and snake myself around his prick. That's how I sit and think.

One of my classmates has come to see me at home. It is afternoon, my parents are out. We lie out in the garden. It's in the 60s. We're not very old. It must be the first time he has touched a girl. We smoke Pall Malls. I am in a bikini, I have a tanned stomach. Arms. Thighs. Tanned all over. He's taken off his sweater. He was wearing it when he arrived, on the warmest day of the year. Now he's taking his shirt off too, because of the heat. We lie for a long time side by side on the green grass.

'Shall we go inside?' he asks. That's because we have kissed. I know what he wants.

'OK,' I say, getting up. He looks at my buttocks, under the bikini briefs. My bottom. He is obsessed by it. I can feel it through the cotton.

I am hot too.

I go up to my room to find my diaphragm. That was the vogue then. The diaphragm cream. I put it in. And go down to the living room, where he is in underpants and nervous. I am there, he mustn't be frightened.

We stand holding each other. I put my hand on his prick

outside his pants. It has grown. He tries to get my breasts out. I help him with the hooks, and take off my briefs. He's got his pants off. We are naked. His prick against my stomach. I want it all.

We lie down on the floor. On my parents' carpet. The door to the garden is open, a blackbird hops across the lawn. I spread my legs and am open. He thrusts his prick in, I help with my hand. One movement and he comes.

He has finished. I am inflamed with longing, with desire. But there's nothing to be done. He has put on his underpants. Now he's buttoning up his shirt. Then he puts on his trousers and finds his sweater.

I lie on the floor. The semen runs out onto the carpet and makes a little wet patch. It isn't dry yet, now he has gone.

I walk around the rooms naked. I put on a disc, Charlie Parker, 1947. I take hold of my breasts, one in each hand.

'**Parker**, Charlie (1920–1955), altosassofonista negro statunitense, caposcuola dello stile *bop*.'

I go down to visit Alphonsina. Jan goes to the central station with me. He kisses me on the mouth, and is in a tremendously good mood.

'Come back, come back,' he shouts, running beside the train. He is always happy.

It's ten o'clock by my watch with the Roman numerals. I am in Germany in an IC train for Basel, and sleep and wake and sleep and wake. I drink Maarum water from home.

Switzerland. Italy!

Smoking too much makes me ill. When I don't smoke I'm nervous. When I smoke I get scared.

I have only tried a threesome once. It was in a waterbed, I tell you no lie. Jan between my legs, and one of his friends in my mouth. The friend had hair all over his body. Jan is very girlish. But extremely active.

We'd been smoking pot, and were laughing our heads off. Then we suddenly wanted to fuck. I must say it's a weird feeling to be slobbering over pricks at both ends. It only needed one up my bum. And a pair in my ears. I had pricks for several days.

My breasts. When I think of my body, I think of my breasts. All eyes are turned towards them when I walk along the street. They're nothing special. On the contrary. They are absolutely like breasts, and that's what makes them so interesting. Men are crazy. They gape at a good word.

But then it does happen that I can send a pupil after a penis.

When I've written a love letter I kiss it and put it between my legs where it's wet and loving. Then I stick it down with spit and go down to the letter box. Everything I see is a symbol. I am a surrealist, see details completely realistically, but it's odd what the face looks like.

A white ferry sails past trailing seagulls. The waves are blue or green. It depends on where you look at them from, and you can change your viewpoint as you like.

When the letter reaches its destination I hope it will be read in the same spirit.

I am poor in money but rich in love. And I can always scrape enough together for a stamp. I take the empty bottles back and get enough money for cigarettes and a strong beer as well.

When the letter arrives I hope it will be swallowed by the eyes.

I flow with the current. Am a non person. My existence is my threads out into the night; I can be inside an electric bulb.

Eat me. Put me in your mouth and bring out the joy of being. It lies just beside pain.

Dread has got hold of my toes. Dread is sensual and clings to my body, up my legs, around my stomach and deep into my breast. I feel it beat in my heart, it pulses through my whole body. And I am it.

I lie looking into the wall. What does it mean to survive? How long will you have to be around before you have lived. I am afraid of dying. And more than that. I am angst. Free hanging-in-the-air dread.

I can always get up and do housework. I vacuum clean. Wash floors. Tidy up the kitchen. Wash up. Dry. Put things away.

Or I am little, and stay lying down.

I am butter; I melt in the sun.

I am a cinder track that is run over by a 400 metre race.

Or I am a teeth-chattering schoolgirl, lying there staring at the wall, deserted by God and everyone.

My mother comes in. She carries a tray of tea and toast that she puts down beside my bed. I don't turn round. I hate her.

When I shut my eyes I can see her when she was teaching me about Tampax. I will never speak to her again.

She makes me ill, literally. She reminds me of nothing but illness. Hot poultices and puke.

And yet we quarrel and make it up. But that's only the mask. I decide for myself, in behind the plastic curtain.

I'm frightened. I don't know why. If only I had a body to lie outside. Or inside. A body. A real body.

In Italy the duvet is just a sheet. It is very hot, and I sleep quite naked. The cool white sheet and the hot skin. I discover my body, I usually sleep in a shirt. It's a fantastic feeling.

Just like the first time you swim without a swimsuit and find out the difference. I introduced topless to Italy. That was something new with my breasts on the way to the beach. Cut-off jeans and health sandals.

I often dream of walking naked through the town. It's odd there aren't more naked people in the shops, on the streets, on the escalators.

I'd love to see a beautiful man come walking by, quite naked, with his prick hanging nicely between his legs. An alluring, sunburned wonder.

My breasts are out the whole summer. They are brown and firm. My nipples can do the most incredible things.

I dream. I'm walking down a long corridor with a cement floor and high concrete walls on both sides. A greenish light comes in through a small window and reveals a big illuminated picture, a kind of circle drawn on the wall in red chalk, or painted with blood, is it? Snakes twine around each other, and out of their open mouths grow little prick-heads. They shoot out and draw back into the snake's darkness, one in each mouth.

I stay there looking at this strange sign.

Then I turn round, and behind me I myself stand with spread legs. A snake is on its way out of my cunt. In the snake's mouth a small stiff prick pushes out and draws back. Shoots out and withdraws.

Now the snake has gone and I stand with my head back, bared breasts, tensed stomach, and cunt in violent contractions.

My hands come up from behind and spread the lips

apart. At each contraction little burning balls drip out, roll on to the floor and burst into flames.

Jan wants to marry me, and I can't help laughing. I paint big weird pictures. They will never sell. And that's what counts, says Jan.

We fuck several times a day, because we want to. I'm glad to be disturbed.

One day we go for a trip through the woods. He's borrowed his father's car and we drive until we feel like stopping. Then we lie on a rug with our picnic. We take off our clothes before eating. Routine form.

We're laughing and dripping with wine. He reads Apollinaire and tells me he's a genius. But I've bloody lent him the book. '**Apollinaire**, Guillaume, pseud. di Guillaume de Kostrowitsky (1880–1918), poeta francese, nato a Roma da madre polacca e padre italiano. Legato ai movimenti artistici e letterari d'avanguardia, amico di Picasso, fu il teorico del cubismo e contribuì ad oirentare la poesia simbolista verso il surrealismo. *Alcooli, Calligrammi; Le Mammelle di Tiresia* (dramma).'

He has to be instructing me the whole time. And I've nothing against that. As far as I'm concerned he can tell me as much as he wants about language. I know he'll forget it in a moment and come closer.

His prick stands straight up in the air. The blood beats in it. I've plenty of time. I can look at it meanwhile.

Then suddenly the sentences disconnect. He rolls onto his side. I'm lying on my side too. I lift up one leg and the prick comes in.

I cry when we have to leave. It's my mother who wants to go home. She can't cope any longer. And I who never want to go home. I walk around the streets restlessly. I can't keep calm. I've tears in my eyes. I refuse to eat. I'm completely dried out. My heart is empty. I'm ill. How shall I go on living without Alphonsina? Without the boys? But Poul is coming home too, luckily. And we lie side by side at night and find words of comfort. Down again. Others. Come. Get up now. And we hold each other's shoulders. I know sorrow will be with me for the rest of my life. I have loved. I am struck down by sorrow.

I sit on top and squeeze his prick. That's best.

I have my *dizionario*, DANESE-ITALIANO/ITALIANO-DANESE. I have a beer-bottle cap. I have my Swiss knife. Red plastic. Red metal. Red plastic. It's on my table. I am menstruating. A sanitary towel with blood on it. And then so much everyday poetry: shit, piss, sweat, spit, discharge, pus. I drink it all. I eat it with a knife and fork. And that's how I live my life. On a little pale blue shelf, washed in head and bum, arranged as porcelain, easy to break. Take care, breathe with caution.

I leave sheets red with blood wherever I go.

In the SITA bus with a trembling sensation of terror of water in my legs. Thigh to thigh, sweat, and faith in the future. It will be all right. There'll be other hours, other erect organs, other mouth corners that suddenly call for kisses.

Far below the sea, and the infinite. I see what I see. What I know. What is true. And I think of Eluard.

'**Eluard**, Paul, pseud. di Eugéne Grindel (1895–1952), poeta e giornalista francese. Collaborò alla rivista dadaista *Littérature* (1919), poi con Breton e Aragon diede vita al movimento surrealista. *Capitale del dolore; Gli occhi fertili.* Aderi nel 1942 al partito comunista e partecipò alla resistenza. Le liriche di questo periodo sono raccolte in *All'appuntamento tedesco.*'

I hold a hand in my hand. We twine fingers. It's eternal. The bus goes on. The landscape goes on. The sun is up. The air. And flies past.

There will be more hours, more hydrangeas, more melons, that talk and talk of a life in a very small town. I stick fast to the seat. When I stand up there's a wet place where I sat. I stick fast to a thigh. I am a part of life.

I am a part of a movement. A rhythmical song that begins and never stops as long as it lasts.

I'm dreaming. I am in a hole. And I want to be there. I surrender to the divinity.

Outside the hole there is a great soft body.

I am floating. I have a big, swollen prick in my mouth. My father comes past holding my brother by the hand. A hand holds me by the neck. Care is taken to get me home safely and not be cut into little pieces by the big knife that mills among the stars like a swordfish in the sea.

When I wake up I am lying in the garden on a rug I have spread on the grass, with a book. I don't get many pages read before I fall asleep.

It is the beginning of a new life.

My mother calls me. It's time to eat. I eat as I've never eaten before. At least ten potatoes, and several pieces of fish. There are herbs in the sauce. I help myself to more potatoes. Drink water, and wine. I am going to eat the whole world. I start here, now.

Then I get my bike and cycle into town. I don't manage to say goodbye. I go to a bar. I stand at the bar holding a cigarette. I drink everything. Then I look around me. I am available.

A girl comes in. She sits down and talks to a boy. I am

in love. I won't give up. I go over to the table. I go home
with them and look at them in bed. I am roused to the
uttermost. From the inmost.

She sighs. He is inside her. His white arse in the falling
darkness. I sit and drink an Elephant Beer. I smoke one
cigarette after the other. He's the one who fucks. She lies
quite still, legs apart. He fucks away. In, out.

It must be my turn soon. I am totally euphoric. She
groans and sighs. He slogs away. I watch his arse move.
The prick that comes in sight and vanishes into the dark.
It gets bigger and bigger each time it comes out. Quicker,
harder, until he comes.

Now it's me. She goes out to the toilet. She's welcome
to stay there. She comes in again and drinks the rest of the
Elephant Beer. She lights a fag, sits down and watches us.

He's ready again. I lie down in the same way as she did,
legs apart. He lies on me, he is wet with sweat. I don't
need to help him get it in, it's already right down. He fucks
again. I use my cunt. Lift my arse slightly and tense around
the prick when it comes in.

I lie and think of her, sitting there watching us.

I cycle home, head sore from strong beer. It's about to
get light. The light is grey, it falls down among the houses.
I cycle quite alone on the cycle tracks, when I get home
the sky is blue.

I get out my key, let myself in and creep upstairs. I go
to bed. I am inviolable.

When I wake up it's the middle of the afternoon. I make
a cup of tea. Take a rug on to the lawn, with my book. I
lie down and read. For a moment, then I'm asleep.

Every morning when I wake up I'm happy. It's not something I've decided on. It's something that happens by itself.

Of course there's the world, and the fearfulness of life. But I'm young. I can't do anything else but live.

I have no money. I live in a small room in the City Centre. I'm not going back to the commune. I'm sure I shall manage.

Now and then my father sends me money. He can't help it. He is ill. My mother is in hospital. Everything is different now.

I meet a boy who's soft. I don't care whether he's the new man or the old man. He's not a man at all. He's a boy, soft and just as I want him. And hard and stiff where he should be, under the soft outer skin. Iron-hard, poplar-hard and as soft as a puppy.

His name is Eric, but I don't discover that until next day. Then I see his name plate.

We lie all night being gentle.

All theories vanish like water when practice steps in. Technique means nothing. Suddenly we don't mean anything.

First he asks me if I have herpes, while he kisses my hand. He wants to know this. I hardly know what it is. Anyway, I don't have it.

He can safely come in and visit me. And since he asks, I think, he can't have it either.

We lie all night being gentle. Maybe we are the last ones not to have herpes. That must be made use of, again and again.

He can safely come in and visit me.

And meanwhile I can take hold of his prick, pull his foreskin back, and lap up his exposed glans. Glans here, and glans there. It goes quietly, rocked in with spit and juice.

We drink water and have something to eat.

'How old are you?' he asks.

'22,' I reply, 'and you?'

'22.'

That is enough, that is all we need. We have to kiss again. On the nipples, in the armpit, the stomach, down to the hair, up in the face, on the mouth, in the ear.

This time I want it in. I rest on my head with my arse up in the air. I see the prick from below, the balls hanging drawn up under the creature, and his eager thighs.

I still can't find out whether it's hard or soft.

He holds his prick and guides it in, right to the edge of its head. It is only just inside. Then out again. Then a little further in. I don't move. Now it's coming again.

We lie down on our side, with the prick still in. We turn round so I lie below, with my legs together, and his legs on each side of me, almost sitting up. I lift myself up a little. I press my mount of venus up towards the prick. I screw it firm with thighs and muscles.

The whole time soft, and hard.

We can keep on. I know he will never come. I begin to feel it. I get a hand in and hold two fingers to the underside of the prick, just at the root, where the balls knock at each movement. I take hold of the seed tube, under the skin, where now, and now, the semen passes and plunges into the cunt, far inside me. I have to scream.

I am the one who comes.

We can breathe again. I try to get up, but I can't. My legs shake under me. He gets up as well, staggering.

We lie down like dead people. Who slowly awaken.

Poul's T-shirt has sloping shoulders. When he lifts his arms you can see the hair under his arm.

I buy shirt-vests with straps. I link my arms round my neck so the sweat shows in the hairs like little pearls.

In the winter I wear an Iceland sweater. One day I go into Poul's room in my Iceland sweater and nothing else.

He goes around in jeans and a bare top. I unzip him and keep my sweater on.

I lift up my legs. Right up to my neck. My cunt is open, right in front of the eyes of an enormous prick. A drop emerges from the crack in the prick-head and falls straight down into the cunt, which is wet itself. The lips close around the falling drop and say: Come in yourself, prick. It throbs with blood and is quite out of dimensions. Then it pushes itself down into the cunt hole, in one movement, right to the bottom. It does not move but is so big that the cunt is almost splitting. Legs right apart. What does the prick think in there? What is it like to be a prick? I am almost out of my mind. It grows. How big can it get? It doesn't say a word in there. Then it comes out and is small.

I have shit hanging out of my arse, and my face speaks. I have my holes. It is fantastic what comes out. And in. I am open.

I've got a hangover again. Not an ordinary one, but deadly. I thank God for life.

To wake up. To know, that life exists. To be. In the midst of it all. To be alive. To be living.

I am, I am alive.

I am my own psychiatrist. I solve my problems with a simple cure. I go out into life. And obliterate myself.

The prick is quite small. The balls lie on the sheet like big independent worlds and rummage around in their rhythm. It's morning. He is not awake, and lies with his legs flat out to the side. I love Jan. He will never hurt me. He can't make himself kill me. He will never stick a knife into my veins. I can safely lie beside him. He can safely lie beside me.

I pick up a brush and dip it in ultramarine. I paint the stem of his penis blue. Then I pick up another brush. And paint his foreskin white. Niveo. His prick is blue and white. He will see it when he wakes up. And he'll know it was I who painted it.

He irritates me a bit with his eternal monologue. But I don't let it worry me. I know what he's worth.

When he gets up and stands there with his gestures, talking about his childhood, the sun and nothing. Nonsense. He has nonsense on his lips, and I run to him and kiss him, right on his tongue.

Then he'll look down at the prick, it will still be little, and blue and white.

He lets me do anything. I take hold of his stiff prick and lay it down on his stomach. I draw round it, almost up to the navel, through the hair. I paint it red, with a yellow line on the head. Then I sit on the real one. And get it well up my cunt. I look down at the stomach. There I can see its red brother, which moves too. But the real prick is bigger. It has grown ten times inside me.

Then I take the prick out, and sit up against it. It is all wet. This time I draw it and paint a red one on my stomach. Then I sit on it again. Now he can lie and see the prick on me, out of the hair, when I fuck.

I take it out again. He is really wild. I find a tape measure and measure it in centimetres and inches. He says: come on, sit on it. He lies quite still. It stands up by itself. I sit on it and rub it off inside my cunt.

Weird. I'm in the sixth form and one of my classmates comes to see me. He's sweet and goes on kissing and holding my hand and between my legs; and I give his prick the same attention.

We take off our clothes and lie down on the bed. Then suddenly he doesn't want to, in the middle of it. He lies down under the bed, he does, honestly. He can't cope.

Next day on the phone he says he says he couldn't take the look of the lips and the clitoris and the darkness and the juice and the hole. He thought it couldn't be true.

I say: it's all as it should be. And if he loves me we can be good friends.

I'll manage all right. I'll sit with my finger in my briefs until someone else comes along who has a mind to fuck.

I am only ill. I'm mad. I'll accept everything. Any kind of boy.

I put my mouth around the glans. That's how I'll stay for a thousand years.

I read all the porn I can get hold of. I've still got the prick in my mouth. I can't come.

At last someone comes to lick my cunt.

'**elettroshock**, elettroterapia per malattie nervose e mentali che provoca violente convulsioni di tipo epilettoide. Conferisce notevole resistenza a diversi fattori morbosi e migliora i sintomi di varie malattie mentali.'

Alphonsina with her legs spread. That's the only thing I think about.

The little hairs on her stomach. And down her thighs.

I can let my tongue play and find a little hair. Then I move down to her pubic hairs and take one in my mouth. I pull the hairs with my teeth, first one side, then the other.

I push out my tongue and slide it up the wet lips. How many times has it passed the clitoris?

We have no need of tricks. We just lie there with our bodies as they are. With our breasts, our thighs, stomachs, hands, buttocks, and cunts.

Both of them are open. Soon the muscles will pull themselves together like a harmonica, and we will scream, in chorus, wild and mad with each other.

We lie on our sides, facing each other. I lift my leg, as I love to do. He takes hold of his prick and rubs it exclusively to and fro in the crack without pushing it in. Up to the clitoris. Up to the clitoris.

Italian fireworks are sexual. They explode and explode, and keep on and keep on, and it rises and rises. It's quite fantastic. To end up with, some real cannon fire.

I've got hold of a book on Tao and sex. By a crazy Chinaman who obviously fucks away like a maniac. It's great and delirious to read about the methods. Nine quick thrusts and one real one. Nine quick thrusts and one real one. The mere word: thrust. It drives you crazy to read about this particular talent to hold back from coming in the midst of it.

My father comes to see me. As I lean against him and kiss him on the cheek I feel his prick inside his trousers. I don't dare think further.

I go into the kitchen to make some tea. Lay the table with white cups, cake plates, paper serviettes, teaspoons, flowers. The light from the window.

I pour out tea, offer cakes. And talk and talk about nothing.

I can't fall asleep. It's so hot and damp that the bedclothes stick to my body. There's no rest in my body. There's no

meaning in my body. It shoots around with its restlessness
and my brain works like one possessed. Whenever shall I
catch up on my sleep?

I get up. I sit down by the telephone with nothing on
and hope it will ring. Then I ring Jan.

He's glad I've rung, but unfortunately he has a visitor.
He's fucking.

I apologise and put down the receiver.

I feel ill inside. For no reason. I can't make demands on
anyone. But why precisely now? When I ring because I
miss him. What does she look like? Who is it?

Is she on top or underneath? Is she fucking too or does
Jan have to do the work?

I picture her. In net stockings, with her legs up. Quite
beside herself, with open mouth.

'More, more, more,' she groans. And Jan goes on as long
as she wants.

He kisses her ear and whispers: 'I love you. You're the
best thing I've tried.' And his prick grows and grows, and
she grabs at it with her cunt and he comes inside her,
and she is totally dead-beat, and satisfied for the first time
in her life.

They will never desert each other, they whisper and curl
up together in the wet bed.

I sit staring at nothing. I can't cope.

I think of my dead child.

I was pregnant. I knew it. I wanted to fuck more than
ever. I had it in. All the time. New pricks, whatever.

Then I was in hospital, after having it taken away. They
gave me pills, several kinds. I couldn't get over the
depression.

When I clean my teeth I use Weleda's Sole toothpaste. I
quite often clean my teeth four or five times a day. It's not

sweet or perfumed. It doesn't taste of peppermint or any 'taste.' It tastes of itself.

'Weleda Sole Toothpaste is produced from plant extracts and minerals in such a manner to render abrasive and foaming agents unnecessary. It removes plaque, strengthens the gums and aids fresh breath.'

Dear child of nature, bring your Bacchus-wand. I'm joining the party. All you need is to go into the leaf-glossed grotto. Here they are all in the thick of the orgy. There is unsulphurated wine, naked feet, naked legs and naked arms. A white cloth around loins and breasts. It can soon slip off if anyone feels like showing off to sightseers.

I'm with a drama troop from Copenhagen. They are looking for a girl with good breasts and a beautiful arse. She has to strip on the stage in the third act. I smile at them, I've downed lots of wine, and now they've brought out a bottle of whisky with the coffee.

I open my shirt at the neck and unbutton slowly until they notice it, they sit and stare at my firm brown breasts standing out from the open shirt, with the nipples right up in their faces.

Then I get up and take off my jeans. I place myself in front of them and take my briefs off as well. Then they get the arse, and I love that. They are paralysed.

Now I must clean my teeth again. I must clean out my mouth orifice.

It all runs out of my mouth, with toothpaste and spit.

I'm listening to a disc by Gruppo Sportivo.

I'm crazy.

It must be my birthday, masses of letters and cards have arrived.

I've put on a striped T-shirt and the shortest shorts in the world.

The doorbell rings. It's the Italian crew come to congratulate me. I know I can get 11 bonks this morning. They'll be glad to satisfy me.

I'm fourteen. I have written a note on 'intercourse' and send it round the class. 'We hope you will find many boys and girls to have intercourse with before we meet again in the autumn. Thank you for the past year, and au revoir. Signed: Headmaster and staff.' It's the last day of school before the holidays. We're all itching to go outside, out in the sun and on the grass.

I sit there thinking of a knout. I lie on my stomach with my breasts against the sheet. Someone whips me quite mildly on the arse with this instrument. They hit me a little harder and a little harder. I am bound firmly to the bed by hands and feet. I lie writhing and scream loudly at each blow. Now the handle is shoved into my cunt, it is long and hard. It is pushed in and pulled out time after time. Then I'm whipped again with leather knots, down my thighs, up my back, and on my buttocks that are all red and welted. I scream and scream.

At last we're allowed to go.

We have bought a packet of four cigars, Alphonsina and I. Then we go and sit in the square, order two beers and light up the cigars. We are near passing out, we inhale so much.

When we're on the point of throwing up we go home and take a bath, and meet under the shower in the longest tongue kiss that was ever kissed in any country in the world.

Then we go into my room. We are still all wet. She kneels down and licks my cunt. I spread my legs a bit and have to support myself against the wall.

Then she gets up, very aroused. And I kneel in front of her. She spreads her legs a bit and I lick her till she is about to fall down in her orgasm.

That's all. We do what suits us. Drink and smoke and lick, just as we please.

We are out in the country. I put my legs up. He takes hold of my thighs and holds my knees down on the sheet, in to my shoulders. There I lie, firmly stapled.

It's snowing. It has snowed all day long and we have been out for a walk beside the sea. If it goes on everything will be covered up. We'll be snowed in and we'll stay in bed for days.

His prick is wet and engorged between his legs. There's hair on his thighs, round his prick, up his stomach. Now he guides it in, I shall lie here like this for hours. I'll watch it getting dark, listen to the wind and the snow. He mustn't let me go, he mustn't take it out.

In the morning we still lie there with his prick deep in my cunt.

When I paint it is clearly not beauty that's involved, but truth. Then it's a question of how to avoid it becoming beautiful. Sunset, terraces and scorpion bites. I talk bosh to myself. It ends up with me getting hold of a recorder and setting it up as rock music.

I have several canvases on the go at once and move from one to another. I think everyone probably does that. It's the same with books. I keep several books around the house. In one I've come to page 40, in the other to page 100. It irritates the others, but they don't say anything about it. They think: don't let's make a problem out of something so trivial. There are more important things to deal with at house meetings.

Jan dies laughing when I talk about art. He hasn't the slightest interest in it. Until he gets his hands on something he can understand. Then it's brilliant. Then it's just the thing for him.

January, February, March, April, May, June, July, August, September, October, November, December.
'I love you,' I whisper. I'm not up to anything. I just want to come carrying tall slim carafes and trays of glasses.
We'll empty one glass after another. The carafes will contain some green, euphoric liquid, and we shall go into a land steaming with dampness and vapours.
You won't hear of stopping midway, you are hooked, like a piece of paper that catches the whole year's snow.
Whoever you may be your voice sounds well-known. Your neck is in water and you suddenly tell me of remarkable intermediate stages in the doctrine of evolution, and on great, still uncultivated areas of steppe or desert or rain forest.
Then we are back again. A couple of minutes or a thousand years have passed.
Now I know your name is Poul. You have Poul's features. And you take my hand and we walk through the streets that are totally empty and white.
Finally we come to a parked car. We get in and switch on the transistor. There is a country and western programme, and we start to kiss each other and eat huge insurmountable hamburgers, while the music plays. We share a coke and a little spittle.
I wake up sweating. Some place between March and April.

My mother's funeral. Poul isn't there. He lives in the States.

God be with him. My father. Jan comes with me so I shan't be alone afterwards.

My father was in the Spanish Civil War when he was twenty. I have been in the Women's Revolutionary Movement for the Conquest of Life. My father loves me, that's indisputable, but he looks at Jan a bit.

It is soon over. God be with her. She lived her life, had her children. I live mine just in the moment. I can't do anything about that.

If the whole lot of them died, I should go on living. Where that is concerned I am completely amoral. I am not going down into any common grave until my time is up.

I ask my father to tea one day in the following week, and say goodbye. Then I leave with Jan. We go to the flicks and sit holding hands, as we did in class four, just before hair began to grow on prick and cunt.

We share a bag of sweets. They taste just the same, and then we hold hands again.

The brain can suddenly splinter. It calls up unexpected images. Then you have to hold hands and bury yourself in someone's sweater.

One morning I go out into the light and suddenly see the whole thing is meaningful. I, who had worked with meaninglessness as a basis. Now I see it all connects. Never before have I experienced anything so beautiful. I know I am the representative of a new movement. Where experience is at the centre, without lies. Now I can do anything. Everything will be beautiful. I can think, if that's what I want. Write. Or not. Love. Fuck. Cook for myself and others. Keep in time to the conductor's baton called light down on the green. There are no rules. It is without rules. There are no laws, but there are patterns growing in vigour.

I am all-devouring. I'm in a restaurant eating starter,

main course, sweet. I am invited out. No matter what he brings us I shall eat it with the greatest pleasure. Mussels, octopus, tongue, tails, necks, grass blades, ground elder, stinging nettles, peaches, pears, all kinds of ice cream, green, brown, white, yellow, scoops and slices, served in a glass or on small plates, with a spoon or dipped in dessert wine and rolled into the ear.

I am a part of the world. No one will stop me from taking part.

After dinner he asks us back. He puts on the television and we watch everything. We are legless, and we watch a Swedish thriller. It means nothing.

I think: if they want to, I will too. But I think he falls asleep over in his chair. And she probably went to bed after the nature film from Denmark. The others have gone.

I'll have to wait till tomorrow. OK, I'll wait.

Everything will be all right. I say that to myself every morning when I wake up. I am a born optimist. I've got some bad scratches on my legs from hiking in the mountains, but that doesn't matter.

Alphonsina has another girl friend. That's definite. I don't suppose I'll ever go to bed with her. And it was silly to arrive unannounced, I ought to have told myself that.

She smiles at me the whole time, as much as she can, but it's not the same.

In the night I dream about her. Couldn't she give me just one night?

I've got lots of money for this couple of days but Alphonsina won't take any. She pays the whole time and arranges the days for me.

I weep. I weep the whole of the last night. My face is all wet, it goes on, my cheeks are saturated.

In the morning I pay the hotel bill, leave a letter for Alphonsina, and go off without saying goodbye *in the flesh.*

The linguistic expression. I take the linguistic expression and shit on it, quite slowly and consciously. 'Art is dead,' they said. That's right, but it lived on. In fact it was born there. Isn't that odd?

I talk to Jan about that. He doesn't think it at all odd. He gives me a mass of theory that just goes in and out.

If I stare at the written paper long enough it turns white again.

Just like Jan's buttocks where the sun hasn't reached. I think: now I'm the one who's going to fuck him, and I tug at his prick. It stands up at once, and I sit up on it with my face to his face. He can gape at my arse while I switch-back up and down on his fine prick.

I feel as if it's the last time in my life I'm fucking. It's the last chance, I think, and suck at the prick with my cunt. I hold my clitoris down with one finger. It's so simple.

He gets hold of my buttocks with his hands and mass-ages them like balls. I'd rather not be disturbed but go along with it. I shall come soon. I can feel it. He scratches my back with his nails. That's just what it needed. Then I come.

He gets me lifted off and up on my knees and enters from behind; now he's the one who wants to reach his goal. He's merciless and shoves it in, completely savage, so it sings, straight on and hard. I grab his balls from below. And hold on to them so hard he gives a yell. But never mind, he likes it, and he carries on with his violent thrusts.

He tears at my breasts. It hurts. He scratches my back and my sides. He holds on to my hips, lifts up my arse and shoves in his yard. Then he comes, with a howl.

It's Jan who fucked. It's Ane and Jan who have fucked each other till they bled.

We lie looking at each other. It wasn't the last time. I know that now. I only thought for a moment that it was the last time, and it frightened me.

I can lie and whisper the word prick into his ear. And he can lie and whisper the word cunt. There we lie making our own whispering concert. We haven't the strength to fuck any more, just now. We whisper, rhythmically, in chorus, in turns.

Suddenly I can see by his eyes that he's asleep. I put a blanket over him and leave him be. I get up, as well as I can, and get a bottle of Maarum water.

Soon I'll have a shower and find my bike, so I can go home.

Blondie. Blondine. Blonde.

I understand Blondie's sound. Quite simply, I've understood it.

Empty rooms with foam rubber, small cutting saws that leave the background free, and then it's the old landscape with the same people in miniature.

I'm sitting drinking a 7 Up, just to satisfy Blondie.

'**clitoride**, organo erettile femminile, sulla parte anteriore della vulva.'

I sit and fall into a dream. I sit and break up.

I'm not interested in the sexual life. The man can stay at home if he likes. But I'm going for life. I'm going for little speeding chariots and Roman poetry, Catullus coming in dressed in plumes and a thousand kisses. Then I love life on everyone's behalf, and cannot take anyone seriously as an individual, but willingly as a partner.

That is not my philosophy, but my life.

I've met a new boy. Now I'm almost too old for the young ones. Not that I mean to be, or they mean to be. But we'll have to be discreet.

I don't paint willies red any more, or sit discussing the art of the twenties. I keep my cool over my pleasures but take them with tears in my eyes.

I'll never learn to live with it.

When I'm sitting down the hosts of heaven arrive in big white cylinders. Outside the window. Like a fire rushing by. I have had my hair cut, and brushed it. I go in for my projects without lengthy reflection. I exist. Let me tell you the wall is white. It's not all a matter of ladders. There's also the horizon, all the way round. The psychologist is a psychopath. There must be a psychologist who isn't a psychopath.

I'm reading about Yves Klein. It must be him who painted my walls. They are all white from where I see them. Perhaps he sees them as blue.

My pictures are not monochrome. I have all the effects in. I am clearly poly-, poly- this and poly- that.

'**Klein**, Yves (1928–62), pittore francese. → dadaismo (*nouveau réalisme*).'

I'm almost done for, but behave as if nothing had happened.

I cycle round town and look at all the white clothes. Have they considered the danger of war? Or do they just hang about, to make the time pass? They talk in very slow voices. They're in no hurry. There's nothing they have to get done. What are they going to do then? I'm ready for their halo. I know what it's like. I have identified myself with their clothes, sent round my skin like an organism, and bent myself together at the waist.

I . . . I walk. Quietly, as if in an infinitely high baby's swing. There are reeds growing around me, thin green ones. My bike is tied firmly to my feet. It is quite small. I can hardly see it at the end of my white trainers.

I love my dreams. They go on the whole time, and run beside me like a prick on wheels. I can dream the whole time, swoon over my childhood, or I can walk as the person I am, straight into the kitchen to make tea, carry the tray in to the table, set out the cups, sit down and listen. I can feel my trousers getting tight at the crotch. I haven't put on Chinese plus fours. I show off my arse.

I'm up in the mountains, with Alphonsina beside a spring. We've got our feet in the water and watch our reflections in the clear stream.

She takes off her white shorts and T-shirt and bathes in the spring. I see her body underwater, in trickling, oblique reflections. Her face above water, eyes closed, and her body flowing down from her throat.

I take my clothes off as well and balance down to her. We're two squirrels, full speed over the stones on the bed of the stream.

The water is cold. We get out and dry our skin in the warm air. We get dressed again, nothing more. Then we walk with arms around waists, back to the town.

It is the nonchalance of being in love, we're in the centre of an excess of it, it stretches out on all sides, clear as glass, completely transparent.

We kiss each other if we brush against each other. That's all. The whole afternoon can go by like that.

When evening comes and the skin has lost some of its heat, we can lie down together. Then the tongue runs and plays its games freely. We arch ourselves, curl ourselves up together, put cushions under our bums, blindfolded.

One day a friend gives Alphonsina a transparent plastic penis. It's not very big, but realistic. We take turns to put it inside us, very cautiously.

It hardly takes up any room, but I can feel it, like a little space ship.

Then I know she will set me free, her tongue will find my cunt and circle around my clitoris. I press my eyes closed and open my mouth slightly. I move my fingers to my own nipples, rub them like two erections. She licks until I can't bear it. Then she goes on a little longer. Everything goes black. And shatters, up through my body.

I take hold of her hips and lift up her arse a little, so she is in a light little bridge. Her lips just in front of my tongue.

Even before I start her thighs tremble in little cramps.

I sit with eyes closed and dream, and feel the sweat coming like water-rolled gravel.

I get a telegram from Poul. He's had a daughter. So he's got two.

If only they feed them properly, is the only thing I think of. If only his wife is on the health trip. Peace and Love and all that. But she's probably not.

I visualise him in a gigantic station waggon, filled with kids and wife and mother-in-law. Before he knows it he'll be in politics, and end up as a senator.

Alphonsina had a white Vespa.

Each time I look at a map of Europe I thank the gods of every pantheon that I ended up in the west and not in the east. I have been an anarchist all my life. I have never believed in totalitarian states.

I give thanks for the possibility of fascination, and for free speech.

I know perfectly well it's not true, but I can still breathe.

I can sit myself in a boat and set sail for the end of the world. I can promenade with my breasts, and with my men. I can buy all the books in the world. If I can afford them.

I know it perfectly well.

But I can't be fagged to buy them. Just like to feel I could, if I wanted to.

That's what I mean by the free world.

And so we have to struggle with it, from the bastions of our mother's womb.

I could go on talking about it for hours, but my father can't be bothered to listen. He's asleep in his chair.

'All that rubbish,' he says.

He's a communist of the old school. But you know all of them have turned into fine academics and businessmen now.

A fly settles on one of his arms and wakes him. He slaps it away with his hand, and looks into my besotted eyes.

I just hate it like that. Worst of all if they smell of booze. That breath, when you're sober yourself. And they stagger around.

It should be like water. Like floating away in water.

I love a boy. God be praised, he hasn't got any hair on his chest, and only a little bit round his prick. But it will come all right.

Then I say to him: just kiss me. Go on kissing me, nothing else. No heaving up great treetrunks. There's no need at all for that.

And he is very small and can easily get in everywhere. He slides his tongue around on me. For hours.

Eventually I allow him to slip in his prick. He's happy and he knows he has to lie quite still so as not to explode at once. Then he moves a little, and comes.

I hold him around his back. Just stay like that.

Then suddenly I want to have a prick.

It grows inside me. He's ready again in a moment.

It's bigger than last time. He's grown a couple of years older. And I lie with my legs spread wide.

I'm not the delicate little girl I used to be. It takes me all my time just to survive. Money's got to be found, shopping done. I clean the house, sit and watch television. I've lost everything.

The sun is old. You can feel it is. I'm sweating. It's so hot I have to stay inside. But I can see it, outside, beating straight down in the middle of the day.

I'm writing a letter. I want to describe my experiences, but forget the whole time.

I think of a snake with two heads, a turquoise Aztec mosaic from the eleventh to the sixteenth century. It is not known exactly when it was made. But it still exists.

It is a twisted green snake's body with a head at each end.

I must buy some stamps too. I'm busy. I am restless. I am in the midst of life. There's more ahead.

I've taken to living like a nail. Squeaky-clean. In the centre of a cosmic micro-macro sails a minute flake of splintered metal. In a swarm of pins flying past. Nails. Screws. Turning nuts, and slender cylindrical pipes.

My mouth is open and tadpoles and plankton swim out of it.

Everything I touch gets soaked with sweat.

I always dilute the booze, afterwards, when I get home, with water. Then I lie down on my bed and everything goes round. My balance has gone to pot. My balance has gone to the pot. It's sizzling. It can go to hell, I don't give a shit.

Then I sleep like a child.

I go shopping at the supermarket. I fill a whole trolley with Maarum water and spaghetti. I expect I'll survive.

I've been given money for a painting. It's two by two metres. It's big. I have loved it as long as I've lived. Because it's filled with polyrhythms.

Now it's sold. It's such a relief, now I don't need to work on it any longer.

I can have a bath and enjoy my own body. It's a long time since I could. It's just before I can't find it. Everything is swimming. I think it's a sign. But what does it mean?

I can put questions, but I can't answer them. That is my method, or fate.

I don't believe in fate. Obviously I'm on the side of human beings, as long as it lasts. There's no point in freaking out.

I'm dreaming. One white wall comes at me after another. I realise they are great milkwhite mirrors reflecting each other endlessly.

I walk towards them to meet them. I see myself in the first, second, third, fourth mirror. I stand quite still with my eyes in one hand. With the other I empty one glass of water after another down into my open mouth.

Water runs out of my breasts and out of my cunt. It runs down my stomach, down my thighs, and down on to the white floor.

One day Poul comes home, and he's slept with a girl from his class. We tell each other everything. He is totally white in the face, from lack of sleep.

I feel tears pressing on my eyeballs, from inside my brain, but I listen as if nothing had happened. I am yours, I think, I am listening to your story. My ears are open to everything you have to say. All my skin is open. All my skin is yours.

He describes her. She has fair hair. She hadn't tried it before. He had told her about me.

I look at him without weeping. We sit eating a pear. I spit out a pip.

Now she'll go to the doctor and get the pill.

They'll only use contraceptives at the beginning.

I listen.

And once she has the pill they can do anything that suits them.

She isn't afraid of the risk.

I sit looking at him.

'Have you got a kiss for me?' I ask.

He comes to sit beside me and kisses me.

I can feel he would like to. But I think: for the first time in my life, I am the one who doesn't want to.

He goes on kissing me. I go into my room.

Then I undress. I get into bed. I see myself in bed. Everything is white. I still have a little colour in my face. I must massage my cheeks. I massage my whole face with my hands to feel I am there.

I can hear him in the living room. He puts on a disc. It's emotional. It's not my style. I must get up. Where shall I go?

I can go into town and see if there's anyone around I know. I do it. I get up. I dress again. I cycle off. There are lilacs in the gardens. And laburnum. The sun is about to go down.

I know all of them.

After Alphonsina had poured out a Martini for her parents she took the bottle to our room and we emptied it in an hour.

You can always take the empty bottles down and get money back on them. I take mine down about once a week. It's enough for a couple of strong beers, a newspaper maybe, or a bar of chocolate.

Then I go back with my prize and open the windows to get a breath of fresh air. A through draught for just an hour or so.

Meanwhile I drink the beers, read about the latest accidents in the paper, and break off little bits of chocolate.

I can look into the wall without turning a hair. I can sit all day looking into the wall.

I dream I'm lying out on the wing of an aeroplane, high up in the air where it's icy cold and starlit. There are clouds, pink and light as sheep's wool, far down below, and in one place there are the lights of a town with its cars and houses and roads.

I wake up in the middle of it. I remember a face. I must have seen a face in the atmosphere.

It's Sunday. In Italy we took the scooter to the beach. I sat behind. Then we had a quick dip, walked along the promenade with wet hair; and rode home again.

Alphonsina paid. She said: you can always pay another time. We had fish and drank vino bianco. Then we each ate a big ripe peach, or a pear, or a piece of water melon with a green rind and red flesh in the sun.

In the evening we might well play cards with her parents, or go for a ride on the scooter.

There were lizards everywhere.

I've got the Maarum water in the fridge. I've bought a whole lot of bottles. It's too hot to breathe.

I sit. I sit and look. That's all. I am filled with happiness.

him

It is a late afternoon. Light comes in through the window-pane and falls on to the white shirt lying on the chair.

He stands before the mirror looking at this face. The vest. The dark trousers. He is in stockinged feet on the soft carpet.

Everything is illuminated by the light.

As he sees the world it is shining, like mahogany, to be touched slowly with the skin. Not to be entered but to slide alongside.

When he moves, he moves with soft movements.

He thinks about what he has missed. Although he'll soon be sitting at a white tablecloth being served with four courses, he isn't satisfied. He is full up, but he cannot come.

Now he puts on his shirt. It is freshly ironed. As white as a powder he dreamed would fall down on everything one day. He sits down on the Chinese cane chair (is it Chinese?) and puts on his shoes. They are shiny, newly polished, although he has never polished a pair of shoes in his life.

He gets up and looks through the mirror, through the wall, out into the trees in the garden. A car stops on the road and he hears voices from the garden path. He goes downstairs, sees his daughter laughing as she comes out of the dining room, where she has cast a last look at the table. The flowers she picked and arranged in the white vase that is as white as the tablecloth and made of Chinese (?) porcelain.

He always remembers the summer holidays of his childhood when he hears sounds from the kitchen.

Every morning at six o'clock he went riding with his cousin in the woods and came back for breakfast. All the family gathered, with big teacups and a landowner in their faces.

Then he went out looking at the small things in the big world. Went to the seaside and did the backcrawl while he floated under the sky. Blue as blue.

Now his cousin is director of an insurance company and he himself is on his way to the hall to greet the guests. They have no domestic staff.

He feels like masturbating, lying under leaves sucking the wet branches, like a flag, but he can't get it off now.

If only he could get that prick of his to come once and for all, but it isn't a film but a fucking reality.

There's a little mirror in the hall and he notices he's lost all traces of youth.

There's going to be conversation, and he hasn't the strength for it. The sentences will come. Into the brain. Like biscuits, or little oval clock faces.

If only he could bang the head once and for all against a soft cunt.

While he's eating he thinks of his mother. When she died, it was an Italian film. Ice. It was all too late. Pistachio. Nougat. No one could say anything except small awkward words.

A fly that kept settling.

Now all that's left is the smell, somewhere far inside his brain, of a bluish milk squirting over his face.

He's in a bell. Hears his own sentences mix with the others'.

Most of all, he's frightened. He'd like to weave a pattern that could protect him from fear.

Even professors write articles in the newspaper now about armament and the accumulation of rockets, but it's not that he's afraid of. Or is it just that?

He has a moustache he once thought radiated erotically enough to send women crazy.

When he was thirty he had intercourse with a bird for the first time. It squawked, and flapped its wings around his body.

He's got masses of time. Soon he'll be underground like a jam jar full of earth worms.

He's wearing a red tie to affirm his allegiance to socialism even though he has worked in the realm of capitalism all his life. He has bought and sold. He can turn quite blue with fear thinking of his defeat.

It's windy outside, but no one at the table hears it. The joint is carried in. His daughter is old enough not to need him to protect her any more. If she has ever needed him.

She hasn't anything on as she is serving, but walks around with her face like a mill and her breasts swaying under her fair hair. She has rubbed olive oil on her light brown nipples, they shine in the candlelight.

We were driving through Denmark one winter's day. And I wondered whether I was a different person. A projection. I felt strangely light.

I was a part of the world around me, and the world around me was a part of me.

He drove, and I sat looking out at the lovely countryside.

I knew then that love was in my heart.

Snow on the fields.

And the gliding feeling in my body of the world.

I was all the characters simultaneously in a drama whose meaning I only began to sense.

He wore sunglasses against the strong light.

I thought of coincidence and felt faint.

All around the globe, and in all its layers and sections, we were like statistics in each other's love.

It was snowing. We drove through the snow. A hint of frost, everything clean in the whiteness.

I saw Denmark glide past. The forests. The fields. Was I hanging up in a mobile being carried through a universe that kept repeating itself?

There were mirrors everywhere in the universal snow.

He sat with one hand on the wheel and a filter cigarette in his mouth. He might have been an American gangster. He could have been involved in anything.

I think of a humanism and a justice. Some breath or other that could replace the gun.

He could have been in the Red Cross. A volunteer in a remote desert war.

He inhales, and the smoke is blue. And grey.

He hasn't said a word for a long time. I haven't said a word. I'd like to know what he's thinking.

Maybe he isn't thinking of anything. I can move all my family into him and he will make room. Open his face while he drives through the soft landscape.

I step into him. I've got a naked body. I stand with arms in the air, legs together, and fall breasts first into his eyes.

Denmark glides past. Small villages. A church among the trees. I am completely convinced.

We don't drive fast but bowl along through the country. Not a word. Only this silence.

I've got a towelling cloth round my hair. I've just washed it. I'm quite naked, and dry myself on another towel.

I am as white as milk. Snow white.

Then I sink down into my memory. I can't remember anything, but I'm twisted out of the darkness like an event.

I'm lying beside a man who walks and walks. Feverishly through a thick blanket of water.

But I'm free. For I have my love. Live on a planet green with grass, where we lie in white shorts.

One summer's day we drove through Denmark.

The first girl he was in bed with wore a flowered dress of Chinese cotton. He had his nose down in her mouth and his prick beat like a violin bow against her thin knee. He wouldn't know what she remembers of that escapade.

It's snowing. It's blowing a gale. The sun shines from a cloudless sky.

It's late in the year. Everything has just begun.

He talks about the new government and social cuts.

There's general agreement that the country is getting back on its feet after the crisis.

It's snowing. It's blowing a gale. The sun shines from a cloudless sky.

It's late in the year. He doesn't believe a word of what he's saying. But he talks, face turned straight towards the light.

He can feel the food calms him. And the red wine beating up in him like a heavy fan. The mere fact of his body being here fills him with a crazy delight. He is not philosophical, but happy. He's got blue bruises everywhere, and guts that twine themselves around his skeleton under the hot skin.

He can remember the first time his son brought a reggae disc home.

Now they drink brandy in the living room while his daughter clears away, humming in her thin shoes. Coffee in his nose. He plays chess with himself. White beach shoes. Rubber. Breakfast with eggs. His wife still hasn't said a word.

What hurts him most is the weakness, when he wants to be strong. Peace is the strongest word he knows. Peace and glass, but he is built of planks.

A whole community engaged in copulation. A consummation of the mirror. He has heard of intelligence services that place liberty in handcuffs. But he can't think because he is gliding.

'Would you like another brandy?' he asks himself, passing the bottle. He has two bottles in the cellar, of the same brand.

He goes down to the cellar and drinks first one bottle, then the other, goes back and sits down listening to all their gabbling. Or he stays and drinks from the same glass the whole time.

If only he was in bed feeling well. In newly ironed pyjamas, put ready on the bedspread scented with lemon peel. Then he could read the same book he read yesterday. About a little bear going for a walk in the forest.

But he's not in his bed, he's in front of the television watching the late news. The guests have gone and he has a whisky in his hand. He drinks it and pours out another, twice as big. Then he turns off the television and lies down with the back of his head resting on a cushion.

The house is in bed. It's midnight.

We are airborne. Bound in with thin cords of air. Shaved with air. And twined round each other so many times, hanging in the air, that we shall whirl in this thread for the rest of time. We are two grown people opposite each other in the air.

Then we share a Carlsberg in two glasses and look out over the sea of air.

Lie in the sheets.

He wakes up white in the face. His balls are big blocks lying on the sofa. A sudden flash runs through him. He can't get up, his prick is heavy as lead, and he feels his balls are about to fall off when he lifts up his body.

He is soaked with sweat, dizzy. He can't bear to have them hanging there in deep steel wires. When he walks he pulls them after him, swollen over the cobblestones; there are shards of glass there; they cut like knives. The sun.

He pours a whisky right to the brim of the glass and swills it down. He feels his blood rush round his body. Whisky runs down his neck under his shirt. There's fire in his trousers, flames lick up his thighs. He's frightened. He can't see.

He rises and goes up to bed. His clothes are on hangers.

He stands cleaning his teeth, sees his pale face in the mirror, like a ghost.

When he's asleep the room turns round quite slowly, like a revolving stage. It's white, and there's blood everywhere. In something resembling a dream he remembers how he discovered that his daughter was lesbian. He came home from work and she was lying in the garden with a girl friend. Through the blood of his eyes he saw them on the grass. He stopped on the pavement, with the gate half open.

Through the green leaves he saw them on the grass. Their brown bodies, and how they knew each other's secrets. His prick beat in his trousers, and he was on the verge of collapse because it went on and on. He went back to the car and nearly passed out.

He went back to the car and nearly passed out.

He went back to the car and nearly passed out.

He always dreams about sex. Always talks about something else. If only he could be allowed to listen to music all day instead of dealing with daft contracts. He has a stereo that's just perfect. And a record collection that fills the whole house. He could always lose himself in music. Off with jacket and tie and down into the sound.

He knows he is incurable fluid. It's the only thing that interests him. And when he thinks, he sees himself as dead.

Swimming. A symphony. Walls of water, like sails against his face.

He hates his house. It's far too big. And hideous, like a memory of every imaginable war. The ruling class drinking tea while its boys are out in the mud.

The worst thing is his wife's new interests, but he won't think of that. When she lies on the floor on her yoga mat.

He can't stand it. She sits on a bucket and sucks up water with her arse. That's how she cleans her gut.

He takes a trip into town. He leaves the car behind and takes a taxi. He had another threatening letter today. He must be insane. Why is he so obsessive about killing his father. First he drained him of money, almost. And now it's his life he wants. But he doesn't believe him. He hasn't the courage to do anything at all.

He pays the driver and walks through the streets. At random. Until he decides that he's wanted to see Gurli the whole time. But will he be able to get it up at all? He shivers a little, even though it is a warm summer's evening. If only he was dead and in Paradise and didn't have to burn in Hell.

He's in a Ford Zephyr weeping like someone who's been whipped. Gurli is beside him on the front seat with nothing on. Quite naked and red from the first sun. She consoles him and says it doesn't matter.

Her big breasts and fat stomach. There's semen down her thighs and she doesn't wipe it off. She wants to do it again, lies down out on the grass and rocks her arse. There's nothing for it but to go and lie on top of her. He stops crying because she's so soft and willing. He can't help getting excited because she's like that.

His prick in her cunt. He hears the cars on the motorway. She groans, begs him to go on.

She stammers breathless words; there's spit in his mouth; she beats her head from side to side, saying no, and yes, and no, and yes.

It's totally grotesque, he manages to think, before he cries out, and long wet stabs of flame burn out in his body, heavy and painful.

She wants it again at once. He can't oblige, and lies

smoking. A beer cap on the grass. Clouds flying above them.

Anyway, he ends up in her street, walks up the steps. There's a faint smell of piss from the basement and he considers going away again. But he's already rung the bell and there she is in the doorway in a housecoat, dirty, he notices.

He goes into the flat and she puts the kettle on for coffee. The sun is sinking. Evening is near. He knows in his body that the town is beginning, but he is somewhere else. He was educated for something else, wears a suit that doesn't go with sleazy bars or a mistress whose only thought is to get enough to survive on.

He coughs because he has smoked too much, and looks at her red eyes. She talks and talks.

Out in the kitchen he sees she's got an open bottle of schnapps, and he takes it into the living room. They forget coffee and empty the schnapps in a flash.

She starts to cry and he wonders if they will always weep when they are together. He leaves.

The streets are running with water. It's rained for several months and everything is saturated and decaying. Green plants grow up between the paving stones, and a smell of wet clothes hangs about every pub.

It's white on all sides. And hot as inside the sun. Dry, and damp. Olive oil down the glass, and hair sticking to the skin.

'You mustn't be frightened,' he whispers, and looks at me as if he could change it.

'Nor you,' I say. And I can see that I lessen the fear with my words.

I read to him from *The devil in the body*, my childhood book. He doesn't read himself, he's given that up. But he likes to hear my voice in front of the fire. Then he lies on the bed whispering, just to pass the time.

White trousers, white shirt. And me, just as naked as the heat from the shutters and the white afternoon sun.

We read together by the light of the fire. Often she burnt the letters her husband sent from the front every day. I could feel from their tone that Marthe's letters grew less frequent and affectionate. It wasn't without a certain discomfort that I saw those letters go up in flames. For a second the flames grew bigger, and I had a twofold fear that I might come to see too clearly.

He walks into any old place. He orders a draught beer. A big half-and-half. When he goes to the toilet the floor is covered with water. The basin is full of fag-ends and he has to push his way through the running stream.

Like oil. Mottled with rainbows and on the way up to his face with messages from a world on stakes.

He pisses and sees the yellow urine blend with the water. Now his trousers are wet too. He walks into the bar where tables and chairs stand in a lake.

A voice whispers to him: come with me on stilts, in a canoe, with torn off hair and hand in the anus. He sits holding a ball of wool and feels somewhere far down in his knee that he falls over backwards and can't breathe.

When he gets out on the street again the road is under water, and it's running over the pavement. People hide themselves under umbrellas or wear big dark green capes.

A boat comes sailing by, full of naked freezing cold bodies, that have obviously been tortured. They are guarded by soldiers from the second world war. He can see their faces under their helmets.

On my sixteenth birthday in March 1918 she begged me not to be angry about a present she had for me. It was a Kimono, matching her own, she wished me to wear it when I was with her.

I was entranced.

I suddenly realised that what had hitherto inhibited me from reaching the goal of my desires was the fear of being ridiculous – being dressed when she was not. At first for an instant I thought of putting on the kimono the selfsame day. But then I blushed for I understood the reproach that lay behind the gift.

It is just a heavy weariness. It is just a heavy weariness.

He walks from pub to pub drinking the same thing all the evening. Never before has he drunk such quantities of beer. He feels himself getting bigger, heavier, he can hardly drag himself through the water.

He has to keep going out to pee, his clothes are about to dissolve. They don't look like the ones he put on in the morning.

He thinks in concepts like directness and indirectness, arbitrariness and spontaneity, and suddenly longs to understand language. The question is whether you can divide up the world into components that satisfy complementary systems? Or whether in the midst of everything there is a centre that cannot be divided and cannot be described by its opposite.

He can remember how he masturbated as a boy. He could sit for hours with his prick in his hand. It was forbidden. Everything was forbidden. And if he wasn't given a beating they spread mustard on him.

When he first went to France, and saw the big city. How could he have survived, boxed in for so many years in a family that knew everything and dressed him in a sailor's suit? Why had he never made a stand?

He arrived in Paris in sunshine, and saw the trees. He

walked around in a bell. Was it perhaps there he went into it? Voluntary, sunburnt. Well up in Marx and the whole of Russian literature. Later he flew back alone, or with the family at the hotel.

He has metal in his trousers. Polished brass bullets. And when he walks it isn't him but a wet Swede with his back hunched up. Driftwood. Rivers out in his arms and down his calves.

Now he's drinking port and porter, half-and-half. He doesn't talk to a soul. He sits alone on a chair. It's a spindle-back chair. He could pick it up and break a window pane. But he sits quite still so as not to move.

At night he lay with his prick as anchor steering himself through his nightmares. Gales blew outside and there were girls on every corner except on his prick. A bird flew without a pilot. Trees shook in his rectum and he dreamt and dreamt of a mirror to walk into, where the other would be hidden.

He does everything imaginable to me. I lie in his arms. He carries me around. He looks into my eyes, smiles as if to a small child. Takes off my trousers, and I've no briefs on. He examines me as if he has never seen a child in his hands before.

Now I say it's my turn, and I bite him and bite him so gently, gently, like a little tooth going into the flesh. Then he lies still. Then I lie still.

I do everything imaginable to him. And he says it's the first time he has been in love.

I don't know why I've forgotten it all. And the new isn't new. I know the whole time that I've already lost him.

His prick stands up in the air. I lie on top of him, with my tongue on the prick, and move my cunt up to his mouth, open, with my legs out to the side, on the white undersheet. He stays still and immerses himself in the cunt, as I move it about in his face. He lifts the prick up into my mouth and I slide up and down around it. Just before we come we stop and lie down beside each other, and come in the air.

He sits making up his mind. This happiness over having been dead, and not belonging to an order. He has red hairs on his chest. He's never been able to bear the sight of them. Porter in his moustache. Blood on his index finger, because he cut himself on a piece of glass when he fell.

With a smile that lasts for the rest of the evening he walks around looking. There's no one to see him, the street is empty. They are all asleep, or fucking for money. It is late before he comes out into the daylight.

When he saw there was sex in the air for the first time he was already too old to get in. But that didn't signify, he had his children, who lay sucking in their rooms.

His daughter loved him from the first day. But she always found other partners. And even when she went mad and lost her high spirits, she never went to him. She had her own comfort. Maybe she talked to her mother?

He ought to go home, but he goes into another place, thoroughly scruffy, and orders a bottle of port and a porter.

When he thinks, he thinks in short sentences. He's always done that. He's never believed in a theory if there wasn't a practice. But it can be hard to be an intellectual businessman and not believe in one's own statements. Not to mention the papers in the briefcase. And the pressing way to the conference room.

He drinks port, quite quietly, and mixes it with a touch of porter.

There's silver in the air.

Then he gets up, leaves his seat.

When he has walked a few hundred metres down the street he can go no further. He is exhausted, dizzy. It's going round with long legs out into the ether. The planets determine, torn away like organ notes. Drunkenness is all around, and a dim grey light that has a disturbing effect. Rubbish. Ropes. Straggling plants.

Bamboo.

He is at one with his actions; he has come thus far in his late night theories.

He enters a chance door to a building in the district, searches for the switch but doesn't find it. In the half dark he goes down the cellar stairs and walks through long uniform corridors. Here, like a gift, he comes across an open door leading to a cellar with a pile of newspapers spread out in one corner.

There's a smell of old sweater. A sailor who once kissed him unknowing. And a vague one, damp, he has forgotten what it was.

He lies down and falls asleep.

He dreams. Quite slowly. About his mother as a twenty-year-old. Or was she 22? He came in in blue pyjamas and lay down, as if in a big featherbed or peace, and she put her hands round his back and held him.

So beautiful she was. And he knew all about it. She rose and took off her night things. He could see her both in the mirror, from behind, and from the front with her breasts standing out, and the dark hairs.

As she slid down in the bed again, he closed his eyes. He was so little, and he crawled up on her, thin and naked in the first light.

She spread her warm thighs, and he sank and sank like a wing in the only thing he knew. She put a hand down on to his white prick and held it for a little while before she moved on to it, so it slid, like snow, into the burning cave.

He was so little, a little pin pressing itself in, as light as a destiny from another life.

She kissed him on the forehead, and he was so little inside her.

Her dresses, always in movement. He dreamt himself in under them.

Instead of killing him his father sent him on a summer holiday. With porcelain, fields, horses to ride and a view over the bay with seagulls in the sky in the sun.

He knew he was dead, even then. And when he came back to dinner he did not hear what his aunt said. He just saw her mouth moving. She didn't know he was a shell. She didn't notice at all that his spine was twisted, and that he could not hear what she said at the table filled with people and napkins.

He never saw his father again. He had left when he arrived back. And he did not know why he died in a traffic accident. It was before the war and family high life was in full swing.

Death took them one by one.

Journalists have written about that time. Authors have published fat books about a world that never was. Tall glasses. Champagne. And men with moustaches.

When his father drove a red Bugatti. Against all the rules. He was already a problem for the family. Even though he resembled all the ancestral portraits. He never sat on his knee but he heard about the family all the same. In the late summer evenings when people were at leisure.

He doesn't dream. For a moment he 'just' lies sleeping. He looks like a hedgehog. Run over by a string of lorries on a highway one rainy day.

The air around him is heavy. If someone came in they would see a person deeply asleep, lying under a bridge in Paris, or in a London fog. On wet newspapers, breathing with difficulty, as if unable to keep rhythm.

He coughs, because he has been smoking too much. He has seen snakes in reality, but when he dreamt about a snake he saw in the Italian mountains; he wakes up.

It was long and kept on gliding past in the green temple nature had built underground. It rushed through him like a light. And he asked himself about his sex. If he had been a little girl he would have picked it up and put it round his shoulders.

He has been under the censor all his life. But he knows he was a little girl when he lay down in the green cave in Italy and rubbed his thighs up against the burning stones that moved and crawled up into him.

He wakes up in his lair. Looks around him, and understands what he sees.

The cold creeps up in him, from his shoes, soaked through with water, to somewhere in his midriff, where he can feel the remnants of what he had been drinking.

He wakes slowly and for a moment thinks he is lying on a beach beside the sea.

He wakes slowly, and sees he is lying here on wet newspapers. There's a foul stench of urine. The only thing he can see is a couple of bottles on the concrete floor and a cardboard box full of newspapers.

He is too old for this. But he cannot drag himself up. He lies horizontally. Like the horizontal. And he starts to weep. He, the owner of an Alpha Romeo. If it hasn't been sold. He can't recall when he last changed cars.

He has a son. He has a daughter. At this moment his wife is lying on a beach in Mallorca with two women friends.

She tells them about his impotence while they drink the bottle of wine they've brought with them. Or they just lie there on the sand and allow themselves to vanish, because they have no more to do on this Earth.

They go up to the hotel and sit outside. Then one tells the other what she thinks about the weather, the wind, the wine. He can't get himself to be their mother or father or sister. All is lost, in that sense. But he can't forget he has muscles that can carry luggage to and from capital cities. He has abstract poetry built into his brain, and into his memory.

When they had fish soup in Rome.

He doesn't want to think about what he has lost.

If only his daughter loved him as he has always loved her.

'I Love New York,' says the postcard. Why he had to desert me, I can't understand. 'MID MANHATTAN SKYLINE NEW YORK CITY.' It is impossible to live alone. 'Night view of the New York skyline and the Hudson River seen from the New Jersey side.' What's he up to in New York when I'm sitting here, with a cup of tea. 'I Love New York.' When I'm sitting here, with a cup of tea.

He fumbles around, lying down, for his cigarettes, and finds a packet.

It stinks of piss.

He is sure he will be the next one. All his friends have cancer of the throat. They walk around talking with their new voices. And their wives have lost one breast. That's how it is, and they keep their spirits up. In contrast to him, who hasn't lost a limb.

He looks down at himself.

He's lying on newspapers. He's wearing long boots, almost knee high. They are soft with hard soles and heels.

His trousers are black with a shiny satin stripe down both legs.

He's got on a dirty white shirt open at the neck. With a pink weave running down, winding through the creased white material.

A big heavy pendant hangs from his neck on a silver chain. It is like a cross, bound into a circle of alloy he would never have given a five pence piece for.

The red hairs. No vest.

He has been drinking gin and tonic all night. Or cold coke, with ice and lemon, in thick glasses.

Little gay boys sit around him on the low chairs. Their hair is swept back and lacquered. In black jackets and holes in their trousers.

He has stood the rounds all night. They just sat and accepted. And in the end they went home with him and slept on the floor with music in their ears.

The latest thing is classical music. They don't want to listen to their own.

One of the small boys wore a string vest. He held on to one of his vases the whole time saying that fascism was a negro doll.

In the end he took off his trousers and fell asleep on his chair. The only thing to do was to ask him to go. But he hadn't the strength to wake him up.

He goes over to him. Takes his face in his hands and kisses him in the ear. He doesn't wake but replies to his caress with a hand on his thigh, where he cannot feel anything. It's too late, he can't love anything but a mythological creature. He doesn't even feel desire at a service station. He can't turn himself into an arse for a teenager on benefit.

He gets to his feet. He can see out of a small window high up. And sees that people are getting going on a new day, dragging around their boxes and waggons of Polish make. It only needs weary horses. And an ideology he himself once believed to be the truth.

All his life he has carried wood to the same fire. Charcoal. He has bought in. And sold. The same goods all the time. And he has loved his children, and their future.

Now he stands here, in the midst of his language, and can't find his lighter, even though he has cigarettes.

The only thing they think about is vegetables. How many pigs they can slaughter. And how they can measure out the earth.

The cellar passage is endless and he still had no luck in finding any light switch. Through the darkness he starts to creep along, struck by sudden grief.

He had dreamt the same dream so many times, about clean white snow, and himself as a skier, on holiday, with the girl who will save him from the repetition. He knows now that it will go on playing like a film in the back of his head no matter where he wakes up.

It's a mattress he's walking on. Ahead lies the snow. And drifts on to a little board swaying in the air. The mattress is full of aphids.

I walk out on to my verandah. My air verandah. And dig a hole in the air. Then I push myself into the hole and send myself off. An airmail hypodermic needle into his flesh.

I wash my cunt, am clean as a postage stamp.

Every morning I count the days. I thought I could live a life in solitude.

They ski all day long. Over the ski trails of the snow.

From the sky they look like two dots. Nobody else. Only the two of them, in gliding movement down from the heights.

The trees, dark green. The white falling snow. The blue light.

The whole world is filled with this silence, that is reflected in the sparkling peace.

He imagines a postcard that will go on staying the same; no one says anything.

The glowing faces, after they get back to the cabin and sit by the fire after the meal.

He comes up to the street and walks through the grey morning. He looks quite ordinary. He's always wanted to mark himself out, be his own man. But he only looks like someone in need of a bath and a krone or two for a cup of coffee.

He rides through the mud on a tricycle. It's red and white and he holds a Dannebrog flag in his right hand. It rises two metres above him on a slim bamboo stick. He tumbles, falls forwards and the flag lands in the mud. He is dressed in his sailor suit, and he's lying right underneath the thick sludge.

I am free. I draw breath in my love.

I am in Copenhagen.

I shall walk in the King's Garden. Sit in the Rose Garden and look at the roses. Then he will sense I am in the King's Garden and take a taxi. Get out, his face reddening over this plan, and walk out in the summer day, relish the sight of all the naked green, walk in his decision, straight over to me. Not to the fountain. Not to the restaurant to sit with a big golden glass of light beer. Straight over to me, where I'm sitting in jeans. T-shirt. Bare toes.

And he will put the newspaper down on the bench and take off his jacket. And roll up the sleeves of his white shirt. And look at the soldiers on guard at the little castle on the green grass on the other side.

Then I will feel love as something in the air around us. And my heart will be wet. And he will tense his bow and send the arrow into my flesh.

His legs are tied up with barbed wire from the ankle to the thigh. He can't walk but is moved around by big boys in dancing gear.

He has difficulty standing upright, but he can't bend down.

He falls, or it's the walls that fall. He stands for several days holding them up. The floor is teeming with moths that cannot rise. Their hindquarters are too big, and they twist and turn, like pupae with little fly's wings.

There is an orchestra playing at the end of the hall. They are tired out after playing all night. They are old rock numbers, with saxophone and guitar. He gets out a hundred kroner note and stands the table a round. He's with his old friends. They laugh and talk of the first swing music.

Pale blue people. Pale blue people. Semen trickles out of pupils. I begin to speak, because I know nothing. Then I slowly speak my childhood out in the dark. Like little lights. I turn in the current, and realise that I live through other people.

He comes walking towards me with big movements, his knees loose, he is hung up in my dream. I am alive and listen to his strange words about a community in water.

His eyes caress my jewels. I resist. I draw out life. Floors have to be washed and flowers arranged. I go around for hours with him at a distance. But my love is total.

I tell him a story about a sister and a brother who meet in a field and part in an aeroplane, never to see each other again. About a weeping that never finds the way to tears, but falls out as snow.

Each in their city. Each in their country. From continent to continent they morse each other with short breath.

I stop in the middle of a sentence.

I discuss happiness, as a concept and as longing. Get ice cubes from the fridge. Lie down on glass.

In a microscope far away an eye observes my smallest molecules – the dance of the atoms. Back muscles, stomach muscles. Thighs that glide in the air. A monkey in the breast. A snake with gaping jaw.

I lie looking. How I walk around the rooms talking. How I'm dependent on *the other*.

Then I stand up and try to forget my schizophrenia. I am not ill. I am a living part of the vegetable kingdom. A movable muscle, that breathes to music. I rub my thighs. I am air. I am air.

As it began so will it end. I know that I shall lose him. That I shall walk alone and think all his thoughts. I have, thank God, forgotten most of him already.

For instance, when he came by car grinning like a boy. And we drove to a restaurant. And he told me about his dreams of lesbian girls on green grass.

Shrimps steamed in white wine. His eyes full of suggestiveness, and candelabra prisms. My sex will be complete. But I shall never get enough. I know it starts as something in the air, but I can't remember when it started.

I can remember my body. Surely that's allowed. I can remember a nipple. And I can remember a hair in an armpit. I can remember Denmark. When we lay under the Italian sun.

I can remember the first excitement in the brain. If it was the first. The first colour of skin. If it was skin. The first pale green, pale brown. And a dark, blue pillow of oblivion.

Then she kissed my hair. Then her long legs lay along mine. And her tongue and mine. And we rolled around over each other, and I felt her hand between my legs.

Our souls resembled each other. We kissed each other's soul. Clitoris. My clitoris. Her clitoris. Clitoris. My clitoris. Her tongue on my clitoris.

He says: 'I'm going to New York, but you needn't worry, it's merely business . . . it will only take a couple of days.'

'It would be better if you stayed here . . .'

'You can come to the airport with me . . . I . . .'

'Here's a cheque.' (He takes his cheque book out of his inside pocket.) 'Have you any cash? Otherwise . . . I . . .'

I look at his eyebrows and his forehead. I kiss him, because I have lost contact. He says: 'Let's go back to the hotel.'

I don't know when it began but I feel it has begun. It will be complete. My sex. My rising sun. I don't care about his travel plans.

It's a play of colour. I can't see what it could otherwise be. I've already taken my clothes off when the waiter brings the bill. There's a tip in the air. A community of beggars. He smiles and bows and we lie in bed without touching each other, with each other right inside our skin. Is that how it started, or had I already lost him in advance? Had he left before I managed to think of him?

He thinks of me. I know he thinks of me. And when he thinks of me, he thinks of me in bed; naked; my summer dress on the floor. How else would it have begun?

He sits on his own with the cold beers, drinking them one after another. They taste of the pleasure grounds in the Deer Park outside Copenhagen on a wet afternoon, where his son told him he had fallen in love.

They walk side by side, round and round. There were rockers all over the place and he couldn't stand the sight of their uniforms. He had just got back from Italy, it was unbelievable that there was so much violence in the world.

His hair was smoothed back. He looked serious. Walked with light steps in his pale summer suit. He had travelled around Europe and loved the cities, each with its night and day, late evening hours in the flickering shadows of the trees, the canal water, or the heat from the yellow walls. He read the newspapers, sat in a pavement café with his legs crossed, and currency for a whole life.

Then he fell in love with a girl he never saw again. He took a hotel room and they just sat and looked at each other. He gave her 1,000 francs and she said she would give it to her mother.

He never forgot her. When he was in a plane, sure it was going to crash to earth, she was the last person he thought of. Then he closed his eyes and felt his stomach being sucked out of him.

She came walking along in her dress, her brown arms, and she smiled as if she knew what he was thinking. His muscles lay close against his skeleton, he was a tennis player who had just had a bath.

She kissed him on the mouth and played with her tongue very lightly, then drew it back. She came running towards him and threw her arms round his neck. She walked with him hand in hand, and weighed nothing.

His son, who was a rebel and wore jeans and a black leather jacket. He stood at a gaming machine with a cigarette in his mouth. He slipped him a fifty, then took himself home. He had had enough.

On the way to the taxi rank he feels suddenly dizzy, and lies down on the grass in a fit of weeping. He's not very old and huddles up in the foetus position. When they find him he has been beaten up and kicked till he bleeds.

He has bruises all over when he goes to work next day. His secretary is horrified and wants to cancel his engagements, but he won't change anything.

'Life has to go on,' he says, feeling grave and a touch pompous.

It is the sixties, he is a man with a future. Many employees. Masses of work.

I stand at the airport and wave.

If he crashes, he will fall down into the sea of air.

I walk out of the door, take a taxi with the last of my money. I refuse to accept his golden cheques.

Now I am alone with everything I don't want to be alone with. Who would believe anyone thinks I am happy?

I sit with my Hell on the back seat and watch the town come nearer.

The streets are overflowing with people, and I'm going into my prison, home to my encyclopedia and a palm. Tourist on this Earth.

Flesh. Longing. Disabling intoxicants. Ecstasy of fear. All packed up together in white raincoats in the pouring rain.

If the police kill me I shall lie in the gutter.

All the mice before bedtime. They tear around in the lamplight. He can't get rid of them no matter whether he closes or opens his eyes.

His whole body is full of soda water but crazy mosquitoes are still singing.

It's beginning. He can feel it beginning again, and he takes his stand and calls out to an opposite number inside the wall.

The concert goes on. The concert goes on.

When he was small. When he was big. When he was born. When he was dead. When he was little. When he was big.

No one must see us. We are a secret.

So when we cycle, we cycle in the air in a secret hotel room. We lie bathed in sweat. We get up, weak at the knees. Can't walk. Collapse on to the bed again, on top of each other, beside each other. Inside each other. Like two gliding hearts beating against each other's sexual organs.

Then he goes off in a taxi.

And an hour later I walk down the street, simmering in my blood.

I got home at 9.30 in the evening. My parents asked me about my trip. I gave them an enthusiastic description of the Senart forest and its ferns, which were twice as tall as I am, and I told them about the delightful little town of Bournay, where we had lunch.

Suddenly my mother interrupted me with a sarcastic smile:

'By the way, René was here this afternoon and was extremely surprised to hear he had been on a long expedition with you!'

I turned red in the face with mortification. This episode and many others taught me that I'm no good at lying. I always get found out.

No more was said by my parents. They were content with a modest victory.

He lies beside me, his feet soaked. On the wall hang all

his pictures, framed in silver and gold. Dead straight, in rows, his whole world of snow and metal.

Human faces looking at us from the vertical, spun into plastic and this particular *hot* that appears as *cool*.

He is a space pilot, who has spent his money on sweets. Where before there were firm walls there are now ventilators that blow in his face with a barely hidden fear.

Black sunglasses as cover.

He doesn't know why his wife left him, but he knows she never left him. She hangs beneath him like an admittance sign to youth, but she left her face in a stone.

He is blue underneath the green clothes. He sweats like a horse. It's the last time he goes out alone to find his pictures. Now he can lie and count his years – and right in front of him sounds the dialling tone for the last round.

At the bottom of the mud lies childhood. He can't see if it is a circle or a straight line. The only thing he can see is a figure who could be anyone, a form that flows out. To anything at all. Twenty-seven commas inside each other, that explode, and resemble language.

The day dies. The light disappears like milk from the liver. All that remains for him now is to advance to the start.

There, precisely there, he sees his grounding, in a blotted out meal.

He sits there, left on his own. His daughter has been inside him again. And now when he lights a cigarette it is because he doesn't know what he is to do with the rest of the time.

He mustn't think of the past; he knows that doesn't lead to anything. And he hasn't the strength to think forward. His life is analysed, but living it is something else.

Where his daughter was, nothing remains.

Let it come to a test, he thinks, and falls asleep. The body is life's resistance. Or, what was it again?

Small waves past the ears, into the mouth. He swallows the heavy spit. At last black exhaustion.

He's asleep. I wake up and see him lying in his sweet sleep, and I'm seized with sudden longing.

Every time I close my eyes I dream of my own cunt, and the prick just underneath it, big, stiff, hard, soft.

I lay my hand, quite gently, on his prick. It wakes, quietly, throbs, quietly, while he sleeps sweetly.

I begin to be able to feel it around my body, and am wet.

I kneel above him with the prick just under my wet cunt.

I hold, quite quietly, his prick with my left hand, so it stands up while he sleeps. My right hand is up in my cunt. Move it a little up and down and get juice on my fingers.

I cover the prick with juice without waking him.

And I start on the clitoris, nice and wet, and clean. Quivering, quiet.

The cunt is ready. The prick stands up, ready, clean and hard, under it, while he lies in his sweet sleep.

I rub myself and hold the prick near me, without waking him.

Just as I come I sit down on it, so he wakes up. He has been dreaming, and sees me, wet with sweat, sitting on his prick, that's big and stiff, far up inside me. He moves just a couple of times before he comes, and I lie down over him and kiss him with my wet breasts on his chest.

Who can sleep in this heat?

I am three people, lying on the beach in the sun.

One whispers to another that life is finished. And the third does not hear.

Gurli, who wanted to fuck. In his mind he sees her before him, very big. She took hold of her nipples and pulled at them. He grew violent, tore at her buttocks with his nails, and the more he did the more she wanted it, but wilder, more.

He shuts off. He won't think about it. Her orgasms, that went on and on, in long shrieks. She wasn't human. She screamed and moaned, wanted him from behind and in front, he had to thrust and push the whole time. It was nothing like his ideas of the sweet horsewomen of his sixth form time.

His life has been divided up into sections of life. Now he is thinking again in linguistic structures. Drawers that have pushed themselves in over each other. His life has been split up longways. Maybe he was a woman, who stood behind the curtain and moved herself into him, and couldn't get in. Maybe he was the result of something that had been tried in vain.

He is a crossword puzzle only half finished. A machine whose heart has stopped, which hobbles over the heath.

There's water lying in the wheel ruts and he has to crawl the last bit, wet through, soaked to the skin. The sun like a big hand, lifting him up and placing him in the farmyard.

He remembers a sexual encounter in his childhood, when he certainly didn't have impotence problems. On the contrary. He couldn't stop. He came, the semen gushed, but his prick stayed there in the cunt, and went on tensed with blood. And the little girl likewise. Went from orgasm to orgasm, with a strange laugh that rolled along.

She had her legs right back. Lay with her cunt like a flower, right there for his wet longing. It was alive, he didn't know what it was that he vanished into. A hand that grasped the whole length, and the stomach that shook like a rattlesnake.

He came three times inside the cunt. He didn't know how many times she came. She lay still, steaming, with her thighs down on the sheet. Her hair, that was quite white blonde, stuck to her forehead. He looked at her breasts while she recovered her breath.

Then he held her by the hips and turned her round. She kneeled up, her head down on the pillow. He put in his prick, which was hard again, as big as it could get, between her labia.

His hand shakes. He stands on a corner and lights a cigarette. He becomes aware of a bad smell, it must come from him. The reality around him, houses, people, rushes into his eyes. He takes a long drag and spits on the pavement. He's like a caricature. He stands there and thinks that himself.

Then he walks down the street, in his cold wet shoes he once bought in Italy, while his wife talked to his daughter about her future.

We meet like rain-soaked England, and I know it's over. With childhood. With my first happy sex. And with the last remnants of my intellectual coconut macaroon in my body.

No more sugar, but love. No more open games, but secret passages, underground, in cars, red in the eyes from lack of sleep.

On a ladder in the air we stand opposite each other, a new life, right down there on Earth.

I walk and walk, with my love in my hand, in the air.

He takes a taxi home. As always, the house is full of people. He arrives with an umbrella and black leather document case with a zip fastener. He smokes a filter cigarette when he gets inside and puts his things on a chair in the hall.

Music comes from upstairs and he goes into the living room to read the paper. He sits playing with his gold lighter. The light, the colours of the furniture, and the white wallpaper.

Food is cooking in the kitchen, children of all ages mill around. A little boy comes in and shows him a grass snake.

They play cards all evening, and everyone laughs at his jokes.

His daughter is happy because her mother and father are in such a good mood.

They sit in a cabin inside the house, and their eyes reflect the flames of the fire on the hearth.

He gets up and goes upstairs in his knickerbockers and sports socks.

He goes into the bathroom. Locks the door behind him. Everything is clean, newly washed, polished. There were workmen here in the spring. The whole house is cared for, painted, varnished.

He takes off his clothes and puts them on the bench, nicely folded. He has turned on the tap and the hot water runs into the bath, white and shining as porcelain.

He sees himself in the mirror. He knows the face and the honest eyes he always believed would win him a place in women's hearts. He smiles at his own idiocy and stupid charm.

Then he picks up his shaving knife. Lowers himself into the hot water and takes a deep breath. As he feels fear entering his chest he places the knife under his balls and severs them from his body with a single stroke.

Before he passes out he sees the blood merging with the bathwater. He's tired, lays his head back.

Behind his eyes he watches a Spanish film he once saw.

Men were being buried in the sand so only their faces remained visible. Then horses were ridden over them.

He hears the hooves coming closer. He is stuck fast in the sand. He closes his eyes and somewhere sees the sky with driving clouds like cotton wool.

Blood trickling out. Skin opening up and making room for the liquid. Relinquishment, like an emptiness that empties itself. A vomiting, or a sudden violent emptying of bowels. Watery, straight from the stomach, through the weak intestines.

On the screen he sees people pushing their way out of a long passage. Coming out on a busy street with cars, mounted police with truncheons, and a heat that strikes him in the face.

Volunteers came cycling from all over Europe.

He wears a gold chain round his wrist. He doesn't know where it came from.

He is afraid of dying. He sees a gaping void before him. A great black box without walls. Without a bottom. He is thrown out somewhere up behind it and falls like a little rotating feather down through the endless space. He falls and falls, whirls around in a sinking in the stomach. Why doesn't he fall on to the cliffs and break into pieces on the stones of the rushing torrent of water?

It is a thin double gold chain that must certainly have cost a fortune. Who gave it to him, and what does it mean, his lying here listening to a record from another century? A crazed noise, and some girls singing like mad things.

He turns round and sees a whole city in ruins. Not a soul. They all died at the first flash. But further out they lie in wait.

He walks through the smouldering chaos and finds a pub that's open. He orders a whisky and downs it. He has nothing else to do. He has talked to all his friends, but the problem is insoluble. The conversations vanish the moment he starts to hear what is being said.

They will help him. Give good advice. As if he doesn't know all about it.

They sit there with their microphone voices and tell him they have always loved his wife. How wonderful she is. And that it's quite all right for her to meditate.

They don't say straight out that they shag with her, but what other shit do they want to tell him if not that?

That he should take himself in hand a bit. Stop drinking, or cut it down to the minimum. And read. Keep up with things. All the socially useful things going on around him.

He once tried to go for a walk in the forest. In front of him his son and daughter in summer clothes. But he was thinking about his work the whole time, and the children pulled at his trousers. He couldn't breathe.

He takes a cigarette out of the packet on the table and asks for another whisky. The world has foundered. Every time a human being draws breath the world founders. And the more they talk about it, the deeper it sinks.

'Dear Ane. We are lost. One day the world will hear about it, and we . . .' I don't read any more, but. Then I go down to the street and I see people, people, people.

I speak to him in the air.
'I learned everything from you.'
'I became a new person.'
'I was nothing before I met you.'
'You filled me with life.'
'I was dead. Now I'm alive.'
'I met love when I met you.'
'Now I know.'
And I walk, in my shorts, into the people. I walk right

inside the people. There are people everywhere, and I go into them.

He goes out to his car. He will drive in and visit his daughter. She lives alone in a little flat.

When he thinks of her life he imagines that he is her, with everything before him. He will be frank next time, he thinks, and get quite wistful over how absurd he is.

He stops to buy a little present for her. He knows she loves white Chinese rice bowls. She keeps everything imaginable in them, in her white apartment.

He rings the bell. She comes out and smiles in greeting. What will they talk about? It doesn't matter. They just sit for a while. She has made tea, and he drinks it as if it was the nicest thing he knows.

He can remember how drunk she always was as a child. A good thing she didn't die of it.

He straightens his tie. Asks if there's anything he can do for her. But she manages.

'Come again soon,' she says as he goes down the stairs, waving with a big right hand. The left one in his pocket. He looks good. Elegant in his age.

When he gets down to the street he sees the town for the first time. He always sees the town like this when he comes in, where the houses have the light that makes them stand in the air, so people can live in them and move away from them, out among them.

He turns the corner. Casts a glance back, and already has the car keys ready.

He gets into the car. Looks through the windscreen at the passers-by. He thinks he is one of them. But he has no body. It was cut off when he went bathing as a small boy. Only his head stuck up out of the water when he swam under the sun. Since then he has walked around with it on a long pole, two metres above the surface of the water.

He thinks she loves him. He knows they love each other. That is all right.

He starts up. Drives out of town, in the dry spring weather.

He puts his hand down inside his trousers and his prick in his mouth. He can't speak, for his mouth is full of his own prick. He takes out the prick, but he still has the prick in his own mouth. He takes it out again, but he still can't talk because of his prick in his own mouth.

It's raining. The raindrops fall down. He falls down along with the raindrops.

Even though he is in a car he is not protected from his fall in his own car. His seed cells are in his mouth.

The sun is on fire. The air is fluid. I can't decide anything in the white sea.

Then he comes to see me with his car keys in his hand. We get in and drive off.

The countryside rolls past. We are flowing. And we decide everything.

How we shall sit beside each other. What we shall say to each other. Where we shall go.

We are always in a car. In flight, if it's not the world fleeing from us.

He tells me absolutely nothing. And I prefer to talk about what we can both clearly see, just ahead, through the windscreen.

It is either the first day of spring, or the last of late summer.

Passion is temporality. Bodies like nails.

Once he had a behind that didn't itch. He can remember the muscles that moved without steel threads. The tennis ball. He picked it up. Stood with it in his hand. And served.

He has varicose veins under his white summer trousers. When he goes down to the beach he can feel his legs are full of lead. He's wearing a straw hat, and he gives ice cream to the little ones.

They know him. Their parents know him. Year after year they have seen him wearing the same kindly expression. And they have talked about the weather, and about land development. The crisis put a stop to wholesale clearance. But now they've started planning again.

They talk of the new government. All agree.

A rainbow ice is not what it used to be.

A rainbow trout is not what it used to be.

And the cloth is not white.

If it was up to him. It's not up to him, but if it was up to him, the cloth was white.

I know he has lived, but I don't give a shit about age and sex. I can see what he's up to from far off.

He loves the abstract, but I am concrete. When I think, I don't think at all. I move my lips, that's all. I make room for sentences, and for spit.

Then I take him into my body. And in that very second he knows what he has missed.

I show him that the world isn't thought. You can't think yourself into spring. But somewhere on the Globe you have the spring within you.

It is neither cold nor hot. But true.

A finger in his hair, and a thigh between his legs. And he awakes in his trousers like a prick.

I have removed him from my face. Now it's merely a

landscape in sunshine. And I can see him without him seeing me.

He moves like a long Sunday up my back and kisses me on the neck. He has spread himself over me with his whole weight, and he has plenty of time. He hasn't got to do anything. He hasn't got to do anything, I think.

So I can relax.

In a year. In fourteen years he will take his trousers off, and I shall be wet all through my body.

I am the one who controls everything. I am not his idea of me. I am the body lying beneath him, on my stomach, in a bed he has hired for a week.

He can't imagine anything at all. I can't imagine anything at all. For now twenty years have passed, and I'm lying on top of him, on my stomach, with his prick a quarter of a millimetre inside me.

He can look at me without my looking at him.

I live on the prick's terms. But it is my prick, when I have eased it inside me.

Now he's my cunt to such an extent that he's given up all his work. Now he may well start to whisper about a life on other planets, and about the great love, I don't listen.

I am as smooth as the sea. I beat with my waves. He intends to teach me to know the whole of Europe. I want to show him where the snow falls on the mountains like flowers. That's not important. I ride up and down on the prick. I ride up and down on the prick. My repetitions are my little secret. He shuts his eyes. It doesn't hurt, but he looks like an angel of death. The envoy from the land of childhood who could never forget that the body burns in the air.

I know how orgasm has taken me before, but I'm only in life for a moment the whole time, and no one can tear me away from our bodies. We are together in the lonely castle. That must be enough.

Hear how my speech closes around his prick when it comes up into me.

He keeps saying sorry for not being able to wait. But he just doesn't see that I was the one who couldn't wait.

His story will go on. I haven't one.

Is it natural for the partners always to stitch their lover's flesh with a needle and chain the other one to a pain that is unbearable? He would like to have the prick back in the cunt, without cross-stitch or a zigzag cutting along the spermatic cord.

He lies on the white sheet and knows he is about to come. For the last time. In that way. For he has had enough. He doesn't want to say sorry and come out with a prick half a centimetre long.

There's a fish hook in his balls. And a little girl in a white forties frock stands pulling in the line. He lies with his mouth open with fear. He has no teeth in his mouth and he has to stand up so as not to fall down dead. He screams. Don't come again. Stay away.

He's even afraid of small cones on the woodland path. He doesn't go out there but stays close to the house, where the adders can be seen metres away.

He stands there with a bucket and spade, in short trousers, and has seen enough. He doesn't dare go back. His mother is not on the grass. Has she gone up with his father? To lie down. Are they lying and licking each other's hands with their tongues?

He is a stake. He can't stand up. And he can't bend his legs. He has to keep his body fit. So you can fuck yourself for a career. And die in a casket of velvet and dead birds.

I cuddle up to him. We lie all night with each other in our bodies. His chest against my back. The prick inside, without moving. Now and again I squeeze myself around it. At first light he starts, quietly.

He controls himself, makes small and long, short, deep thrusts. He goes on. It's the best thing I've ever tried.

I'm sweating. He means to go on for the rest of his life. I have never been so happy.

We are at a hotel in Germany. What a place. Outside the children are going to school. Now they're coming home. The walls are green, and reminiscent of some schoolroom doing geography or zoology with stuffed animals and snakes in spirit.

He's on his way. By car. Home. But at the same time he's sitting in a cafeteria drinking coffee with Gurli.

She has her own way of being human. She lives from day to day. She trained as a psychologist, but never practised. Her student exam was mentioned in the newspapers. And she has lived in Christiania, the squatters' city in Copenhagen, selling beer.

He has a feeling he loves Gurli, who is always drunk.

When she's drinking coffee she has one cup at a time and talks about her experiences. He drinks the whole jug in one go, and doesn't say a word.

That's why they haven't had children. He's uneducated, but dreams of a way of being together.

He had a car and a cheque book. She had an inestimable lust. She has no money and is always searching for a five pence piece. Maybe she'll find it one day.

It won't be flat but ball-shaped. She'll gulp it down and never swallow again. For she is satisfied with him as he is.

They ask for extra cream. But they have to go and fetch it themselves.

Then they drive out into the country and sing a song only she knows. He can't go with her into romance. He has enough to do keeping the spiders at a distance.

He's brought a hip flask with him. They pull up at the side. But before he can get it out she has taken off her sweater and sits with her breasts out.

Then he kisses her on the mouth, and holds one breast with his hand, which starts to shake. He would like to just be the milk. But he has stars on his neck and suddenly falls on her.

She has a hand inside his trousers and wriggles her briefs off. When he puts a finger in, it is wet.

They can't manage, and they can't wait. With God's help they get it in on the back seat. They can barely move but she doesn't care if only she has him inside.

Then they lie down out on the grass. Take off the rest of their clothes so they have free play.

It's late autumn. All the birds have flown. He'll never do it again. Bring children into the world and look after them. Start a circus again.

He's smoked so many cigarettes he can hardly breathe. He's seen the packets burn up.

One day Gurli will have no breasts and be unflinching. The whole community talks of nothing else. If a community can talk. It's prosthesis from morning to night. And his body is intact.

Our age has been wiped out, and that we know each other. The whole of the past and the whole of the future are concentrated in the clitoris, and vanish at the moment he releases the seed and it drives into me, in a spray for life.

I have forgotten what he has said to me over the years. He has forgotten what I've said. And we don't intend to say any more, ever, to anyone.

Berlin. It's like a rock disc. He's not interested in rock. I tell him with my skin that we've landed up in Berlin.

Then I lie on my back and lift up my body in an arch. I have unfolded the water lily, and he comes with his sword-fish and rips me up.

He remote-controls his television set. There's no one at home, and he can drink as much as he likes. If there was a pornographic film on he would switch over to that. Or a programme of music for the young. But all there is is a schoolteachers' discussion and a film that speaks for itself.

He hasn't any yoga for that.

The moon is out. And he thinks about the human being again.

Music as music, isn't that an idea? He would like to have seen his son in love. But he always kept to his sister. Whatever obstacles that might cause. As usual he doesn't understand anything. It will end up with his being proud of that although it wasn't what he wanted.

His wife once told him the meaning of life. But he forgot it.

Three cigarettes left. That's nothing. He'll have to go into town again. Luckily he finds a packet in the car.

The wonder of repetition. The smooth porcelain of repetition.

Green grass. White butterfly. And a love machine that lasts all life through.

I read everything that's sent me, in Danish. So when I get home I'll know everything about women's orgasm, men's orgasm, basic groups, dreams, fractions.

I fly like a white butterfly over the green grass.

If you once start to make a study of life there are no limits to what you can discover.

But he just sits in his chair. Because he won't go out. Each time he's made a move he's come back like one dead. So why go on? And yet he gets up in the morning thinking that it's a new day and a new time.

He's taken off his jacket and sees a maggot on his right sleeve. Has it hatched from an egg in his shirt, or has it been put there, now, to fill him with horror? He sits perfectly still looking at it. Anything from nature sends him into a fright.

Then he walks, and each leg is made of wood, into the kitchen. He lies down on the floor and promises himself he will never again come home drunk.

He had an idea of an architecture filled with people. Before he himself went into business. But he has it still, in the midst of disgust from all sides, and the new rock, which he is well aware comes over the loudspeakers. It's just that he can't communicate it. As they say. And he lies with his head in the dog's bowl.

Tomorrow he'll sell his job. He bloody won't. But he'll never go there again. Of course he will. He'll be sitting there again tomorrow.

With both hands on the desk. And a secretary who'll say good morning. Whatever she means by that. All she's after is money. For the rent. And the parrot. He can't cope with it.

The ideal requirement. He who had an ideal requirement. Now he only begs for a dog biscuit. And a tad of silence from the staff. Belt up with your ideas of a new society.

He loves me. It's no lie. He brings gifts, and sits, even if he's thinking of something else, for hours talking of the craziest things.

Sentence-forming is like the body, like flesh that's alive.
Or like Miles Davis in Paris, with his trumpet right out in
the night.

I can sit and dream things up even if there's no reason
to invent.

He loves garlic. A couple of cloves in the salad every
day.

He wears a tie even though I've told him it's not smart.

'I don't give a shit whether it's smart or not,' he says,
and can hardly pronounce the word.

'But it really doesn't suit you,' I say. 'You'd look better
with a bare top, or in an American T-shirt.'

'Bare top,' he says. That's all it needed. He rolls over on
the floor and looks like an actor in a film. He loves to lie
on the carpet feeling free.

He took LSD in the States. And smoked hash. Drank
everything he could find.

If he'd got some good grass I'd be glad to smoke it with
him. But he asks me the whole time if I don't know someone who has. But I am outside all groups, as he well knows.

He loves slightly crazy talk, and seriously crazy things
on TV, when he sits in front of the screen and believes
everything politicians say is lies.

'LSD is not something to mess about with,' he goes on,
even though I only drink mineral water and sit quite still
with his jacket round my shoulders in the cool of evening.

'Miles Davis,' he says, although jazz has never been his
strong point. 'Miles Davis, now, he's something else.'

'I don't give a bloody shit,' I say, and in a flash I've got
hold of the zip in his white sailing trousers.

He lies with his head between my legs and I have my
hands in his hair. He knows me completely, and I don't
need to brood over anything.

He licks my stomach. Kisses, with his tongue, all over. I
can't keep quiet.

His prick against my thighs.

He sits up so the prick stands before me.

I free myself and sit up on it.

He loves me.

He goes to Rome. Suddenly he's standing in the Termini
at 25 years old. He's his own son. He sweats in the heat.
His aim is to join the Red Brigades. He has convinced
himself and there's nothing more to discuss.

He has analysed society. Talked to everyone about his
'problems'. There is no problem. That's the truth. For there
is no other way out of suppression. All of history is witness
to that. Once you have looked at events from a distance,
there is agreement. The only thing they can't stand is a
little blood.

They are only innocent on television. It is them. They
have taken over creation. They could have let well alone.
And believed in their own youth. They themselves talked
of justice. And went to the pictures with their sweethearts.

He drags a strange boat through the mud. He is a twisted
rope, a thread from the sky. And behind him this vessel
sails through the water in the streets. He doesn't dare turn
round. A large boat, only a half metre behind him, full of
children, dying, and pricked by Vietnamese straw. He has
had this boat behind him for so long that he can't remember what he's forgotten.

He hears a rock orchestra from an open air concert and
for a moment thinks it is Wagner over a synthesiser. He's
got booze on his arms. And blood down his chest. He
himself pulled the water up under the boat but he doesn't
know where he started.

The whole of Rome is under water. It's pouring down.

All the squares are sailing. The fountains piss out into the great lake. He sits on a piece of paper. It is his contact with The Christians. For a moment he thinks that as a boatman he is excused. But now he hears from a loudspeaker that it's him they are after.

He will lie in a Fiat, in the boot. In his own blood. As he was born, with a placard marked The People, and with an apple in his mouth.

What's the time in the afternoon? He doesn't ask me about anything any more, and hasn't got a guilty conscience. We can go on.

We masturbate together. He is mad to see me masturbate. Is there anything in that?

Then in return I want to see him. Grown man masturbates for his beloved.

Then it's evening and we go down to eat lemon sole.

I shall never forget these days without meaning.

He admits it. He accuses himself. But it's too late. And he sees his daughter sitting in a pavement café in the sun.

She has a cigarette in her hand. And in the other hand she holds his gold lighter.

She takes out one cigarette after another and sends them floating on the current past the crowds of people moving in the same direction as the wind, that wakes up all the children in all the windows. They sit smoking, quite small, on their mothers' arms.

For a moment he thinks Rome is the centre of the world, but discovers that he's in a plane drinking what is served. He can hear he is high above the Earth, where he was used to living his life.

He sits out on the heath and hasn't any semen in his sexual

organs yet. He has no responsibility for anything. He is too small. And no matter what they say he can't fuck. But he can come.

He has a bow. And a first fear wells up in his stomach, that he will never drag himself out of even if he smokes himself to Hell and burns in the thin knots of sewing thread. He has an arrow in his heart. And he sees his first friend holding it in his hand, like a bloody remnant of his mother.

It's good that he can just go out and take the bus into the city centre. Everything is free in this town. A couple of hundred lire and you can go from church to church.

He eats a meal fit for a king. A young lamb has lost its life, and he sits holding something resembling a fork, in his right hand. In the left he holds the knife that cuts the flesh into pieces.

He is the princess of speech. Every time he opens his mouth the clitoris comes out.

He wants to go home. A varicose vein has pushed through his trousers, so the hotel can see it. He can't sleep because he is the only human being on Earth. And yet he knows he is only a molecule. A star in the sea of stars.

He is not far from home. Gurli is with him on the piazza. Then he leans over the table and lays his newly ironed hair down in the music. She gets hold of his untidy hair and notices that the semen is on its way up under it.

It looks like that in reality already. A pole that falls over, and inside it a little child.

When he's asleep he looks different. I get quite frightened of what he is up to.

One day I'll start to paint again. Then I'll shut my eyes and say shit to the whole thing.

Gertrude Stein and her aphorisms.

No one knows that they are the only ones. They could dance if he didn't have poles in both legs and can barely get up after the triple Stock. The waiter can't carry the tray, he passes out on the way in and knocks over a violin playing Brahms, while the water slowly changes colour and is now the boat's wake.

In reality he has been saying Gurli all his life, but now he's going to be punished. He knows it, and carries his racket to the net.

If he was sun-tanned. If his thighs were red from a cycling trip in Denmark. But he doesn't deserve it. He lies under the surface and stammers out what was once stammered in his ear. When he could hear. And was ordinary besides. But it cost a charter flight which was never repaid.

He is wearing his suit. He is what could be called handsome. If he was younger he would have had an ear ring on. But he listens to Beethoven. He's not interested in his children's tastes. Even though he loves them.

He has never tolerated the least aggravation, but he has liked to see the world as a new world. He knows that in his own way he is beginning to seem comical. But he goes along with that.

He has shut off all the radio news programmes. Switched off all television attacks on the last bastion. But here and now he knows that he's sitting with himself on his lap, and will never get his wife back from the East.

If he hadn't gone off travelling he might have been able to hold on to his balls. But he knows that the binge he once saw as the first, will also prove the last.

Imperialism is only a symbol. As an adult he knows that he's true blue. He can never shoot himself from all sides, but he can drive a car from one end of Europe to the other and speak to a person who is not sitting beside him, in the light falling in through the window. The most he can do is to leave the car and walk.

And when he has taken off his clothes and stands right under the fountain he will be hard pressed to smell his own blackness.

He sees Gurli, sober suddenly, in big pyjamas. She picks him up and puts him on her hand.

One can speak of different degrees of madness. But we are really just as much a part of the world as so many others. We now are in the midst of our love even though doors are open in all rooms, and it's cluttered with Chinese vases and flowers and water on the carpets.

He lies beside me in his pure, simple sorrow, like a lady's hat I once saw in Copenhagen. There was light from the sky and I couldn't help looking at this work of art, winding straight out of the flowering trees.

It has nothing to do with my dreams, for I have moved myself out of myself, and live the whole time, careless of whether I have lost the comprehensive view for a moment, or overlooked it. I don't care, for it is nothing to do with me.

Who was the young girl he dreamed about? Even before he had met any, and was lying in the blue, floating darkness. Where only a yellow light shone. What was it he wanted with skis down his back? And a snow he had never seen.

Tall plants grow up in the thin night.

He has the whole family inside him, like a starfish. And he has seen a hare hung.

How can someone die and still go on living? He can ask himself that as he is falling asleep.

When he has piss on his fingers he knows it comes from his nearest surroundings. He can't get up without falling down into an indefinable fluid, he knows from his first years in the office.

And even though he's drunk, he can get his bearings. He's only a human being, but he can still not understand why his shoes are wet, and smeared with a red roe he has never asked for.

The vacancy of time. The big hand.

We want to turn the world into images. In that sense we are a couple.

The solitaire of action. We won't come out, for we are merely counters, jingling coins.

I dream about his shoulder, that I lie on when I fly. Features run down the body and disappear into the dark. The eternal standing prick.

I must be a Japanese. I feel so Japanese between my legs. I want to drive my space ship to the stars.

The choking feeling just before orgasm, and then liberation. The Tokyo traffic, and an ankle with silver bells. Legs up, body filled with needles, and glass that leaps from the clitoris up to the brain.

We walk together under the palms. When he says something to me it sounds like a bird flying past far away over the horizon into the distance. There are mirrors everywhere, in the universal snow.

I see our life on every street corner. And I am happy, right out to my nipples, when I dive into the blue sea.

We lie on the beach, under the sun. Does anyone see I have my hand in his trousers? Now I'm wondering how I can get him back to the hotel room as quickly as possible, behind the shutters, in the shadows, on the white sheet.

We are under the shower. It has a hard on again.

We don't manage to dry ourselves. I lean over the basin, back swaying, he takes hold of my buttocks, they're dripping with water, the prick head is in, and we stand still, for a long time, a little further in, small wet movements, I see him in the mirror, he sees me, watching him, in the mirror.

His face, he opens his mouth, he tries but he can't keep his face still. One or two quick movements, he shuts his eyes, and I watch him, I'm not joining in.

Wet as Japanese fish we lie down on the bed. He licks the water off me, but everything stays wet. It's hot and I lie on my back. He gets down to my thighs and suddenly his tongue is in my cunt. Finding its way up and around, back, carefully and all the time.

Then I think: we'll stop the film here, right now, when the muscles start, and the stomach, and he goes on, the clitoris is gone, I am gone, he is gone, the hotel room is gone. Only the water runs down the body and I stand on a bridge, high up, and hear the sound, that gushes, beneath me.

I pull him up and before he knows it he is inside. He sweats, the water evaporates.

Then I feel how he's fucking, only with pleasure. Outside the blossoming cherry trees, the eternal snow. The world's fastest train, millions of people.

It's incredible the way I can come. I decide it myself.

Haikus on my nipples, a temple on my stomach, marching armies in the softness of the cunt.

I put my arms around my neck, he raises himself on his hands, face to face, open eyes, nothing is secret between us. Except what our names are, who we are, why we are; why are we?

We want to turn the world into images. Go out into it and hang up glass everywhere in the heated air.

He wakes up. In a cold sweat.

He goes into the kitchen. Walks from room to room. Why is no one at home?

The least they could do is to be at home when he is frightened. Alone and afraid.

His shirt is soaked with sweat.

He goes up and changes.

He hears sounds below. He goes down and looks round. No one. Then he hears sounds upstairs. He goes up again. There's no one.

He sits down. But he can't relax. He walks around restlessly. In the kitchen he stands looking out of the window.

Now he wants to take photographs. But I put a stop to that. What does he want with pictures of me with no clothes on?

Then I say to him, we are in the realm of love, and there are no limits to be drawn here. So if he wants to take pictures of me, shoot away.

And he takes out his camera gun and sends one stunning salvo after the other into my flesh, and I twist myself in my body and can feel nothing as he gradually forces his way in.

'When I was a child.' It's just before I start to forget. But then I remember, and talk about the waves outside the window, the white speedboat on its way over the sea, and that perhaps I may possibly be pregnant.

But he doesn't believe that, and runs up to embrace me. Stands outside with his saxophone playing a long, meaningless solo.

He hasn't got a saxophone. He doesn't play solo. I am not in the least pregnant. I take my pill. He bashes away with his photography.

When he gets home he has a feeling, as soon as he puts his key in the door, that there's someone in the house.

There shouldn't be anyone there.

His daughter moved out several years ago. And his son has been a handful ever since he 'beat it', as he called it, when he was still at school.

His wife is abroad.

He walks around the house with this weird knowledge that he is not alone.

He put his things down in the hall. It's summertime. He wasn't wearing a coat. He keeps his jacket on, and his tie. He doesn't know why. Maybe to feel protected against an unknown threat.

He jumps violently when he hears a loud noise from the hall. He rushes through and there to his great astonishment and dismay sees that the mirror is shattered and lies on the floor in a thousand pieces.

No one is there to have broken it. It has shattered itself.

He has read about this particular phenomenon, certainly, but hadn't imagined he would ever experience it himself.

He goes into the kitchen for a dustpan and brush and a newspaper to wrap the largest pieces in; but as he opens the door he realises his feeling was correct. He is not alone in the house.

Before him stands his son. That's the worst thing that could happen, he manages to think, before he sees there's a knife in his hand. It's the sharp kitchen knife, an instrument he uses on the rarest occasions and then with the greatest respect.

He stands paralysed trying to work out how to talk sense into him.

But it's too late. He has already lifted the weapon and plunges it with all his strength into his chest.

He falls down against the wall, and as the blood gushes

out and colours his shirt, the knife stabs him again, this
time in the stomach.

He sinks to the floor. The pain dissolves into uncon-
sciousness.

His son goes on stabbing him long after there is any
meaning in it.

He is not after his wallet, or anything else of value. He
kicks him once in the face, that has been sprayed with
blood, and leaves.

As he walks through the hall there is a crackling under
his shoes, and he sees the floor is covered with small
fragments of mirror. The frame still hangs on the wall.

His son has disappeared.

*One afternoon I found a young airman with her. It was her
cousin. I refrained from using the familiar pronoun for her, but
she came up to me and kissed me on the neck. The cousin smiled
at my embarrassment.*

*'My dear friend,' Marthe said to me, 'you mustn't be afraid
of Paul, I have told him everything.' I felt shy but at the same
time delighted that Marthe had told her cousin about our love.
This charming but superficial young man, who had no thought
for anything besides his uniform, was thrilled over our adventure.
He looked down on Jacques, who was neither an airman or a
professional pub-crawler, and thought we were playing a nice
fast one on him.*

I put down the book for a moment. I'm crying for joy. I
can feel I'm starting to get hungry. I get dressed and sug-
gest we go down for something to eat.

He orders the dearest red wine on the menu, and looks
dead elegant in his white trousers, white shoes, white shirt
and blue sunglasses. If I didn't know better he might be
my son and I a cousin of good family who had taken him
out to show him one of the better places.

The kitchen is full of water, like an aquarium. Through the window he can see the garden. He lies in the water in his suit, like a board pressed down under the surface.

He rocks up and down but is unable to bend or arch his back. He discovers the whole kitchen is red with blood, but that the water he lies in is clear.

In a way that's inexplicable to him he is moved through the water, at a varying height from the floor, without bumping into the wall or objects in the room.

He looks down at himself. He is impeccably dressed, in newly polished black shoes, decent suit, white shirt, jacket buttoned up, tie. His hair, combed back, is in the water. A touch of white at the temples.

He sees himself, as he lies in the water.

He looks down. On the floor, clean of blood, lies the dangerous sharp kitchen knife he always treats with the greatest caution. Everything else in the place, the walls, the floor, the kitchen table, are covered with blood.

His son has disappeared.

His son, who came by, uninvited, and stabbed him down with the knife. After the hall mirror had shattered, when he was on his way to the kitchen for a dustpan and brush; and a newspaper to wrap up the biggest pieces in.

He begins to remember. He realises that he hasn't forgotten anything of what he had remembered in the course of time.

He is taken through the kitchen into the hall; it too is full of water. And further on, into the living room. Into the dining room, where, to his instant amazement, he sees the whole family gathered round the table, sitting there eating with napkins on their laps.

There are guests. His daughter is serving. He can't hear what they are talking about, but he can see his daughter smile, as if she is thinking of someone else.

Has she succeeded, in her life, in uniting herself with the reflection; in always being what she herself would call happy? When she goes around in her solitude is she perhaps in a dream, in which her other half has taken up residence. Where she knows no loneliness because her complement is no longer her complement but a part of the globe.

He thinks, and he discovers that when he thinks he knows immediately what it is he is thinking of. It is as if the water around him already knows what he wants to think and has thought it for him.

It presses lightly around his skull, like a hand supporting his neck; lifts him when he wants to see.

The guests have left. His wife yawns and suddenly swallows a little green fish that came swimming through the water. He sees her moving it around her intestines with the greatest of ease. To and fro, as if to music. A warming up programme before she prepares to meditate and shines like a lamp in the water.

He goes out into the conservatory, where brother and sister are giggling over something he can't guess at. A joke? A love he doesn't know exists? An association for the eradication of loneliness from the world? Or are they about to sleep together? Isn't her hand inside his tight trousers, while he splutters with laughter? Hasn't she spread her legs to make room for his tongue, which lies around her clitoris as she groans and leans her head back? She unbuttons her thin Chinese cotton shirt so her breasts come into sight. She is tanned all over. Her nipples are pale brown, and stand up when she arches her back.

If he shuts his eyes he sees the same thing.

He discovers that he does not decide for himself. That

the water pulls a strip of film in through his face and presents these images, incessantly, like reality itself.

He is in a bell. Sunk down into this water. He can't hear the music. Is there any music? But before he can think to the end of the sentence, a whole orchestra is inside his head.

His skull is a gigantic mussel shell, in which the orchestra has taken its stand. The conductor turns round with a hand to his face. Then the sound strikes up, like a thud in the neck. Everything in him bursts into smithereens, his balls fly into space like little shards of mirror. The sound is like a nail through his skull, holding him fast. All that remains is his head, tethered to the floorboards. The rest of his body hovers above him, like an ice lolly among the stars.

Shit, if it isn't one of those yuppies in bermuda shorts and LaCoste top coming over to blather, while we sit hand in hand under the table. Pale blue and pale yellow, and my back stiffens. I don't know how you can be friendly and wish to kill. I always go along with it and reply to daft questions and continue the conversation instead of shooting off the killing look immediately.

At last we're alone again, and I don't know how we can recapture the silence at the table.

We can't calm our bodies down all evening. He talks, I talk, of one futile subject after the other. About our world, our doings. About sugar and lemon and crème fraîche and flaky pastry and iced tea and whatever.

Ballet. Broken legs. A whole life wasted.

He comes walking along in a boxing ring. He is tied to all four corners and can only take one step forward and one back. There's a starfish on top of his head. He is in swim-

ming pants. It's 1945. Peace is the same as a fuck in the
heather. But he can't get there.

He walks around the rooms. Hears noises from all sides. He
goes upstairs. Nobody there. He goes down. Not a soul.
He hears sounds from the conservatory. From the
kitchen. He can't calm down. He switches the television
on and off. There are sounds in the garden. He gets up.
Sits down. Is there someone at the door? He goes into the
kitchen.

As he thought. He wasn't alone. He had a feeling the
whole time that there was someone in the house.

In front of him he sees his son, in a black leather jacket
and the eternal jeans. He has a knife in his hand. The most
dangerous one in the house.

So he really meant the threats. He thinks. Slams the door
and runs as fast as he can into the hall and upstairs.

His son is after him. He rushes into his bedroom; there's
a phone beside the bed.

But he doesn't get far before his son has driven the knife,
with all his strength, into his back. His breath goes, he
crashes to the floor like a dead man. His son sees him in
the mirror, and in reality. He stands knife in hand. Then
he kneels down beside him. He looks at him and thrusts
the knife into him, again and again.

At last he throws down the knife. It lies on the floor,
covered with blood.

His son has disappeared, downstairs with quick steps,
out through the hall. On all the little splinters of mirror
scrunching on the floor, he sees red blood. He slams the
door and is gone.

I know quite well that I can run upstairs and that he can

catch me if he doesn't walk on to sit and read a paper in a foreign language.

How long we'll have together is up to life. We are prepared to be the world's happiest people, we are not the ones who make wars and dole out food in refugee camps.

While I sit in a chair dreaming I forget all about my love and think of a girl I was once in love with.

She had the thinnest silver chain in the world round her ankle, and when we lay side by side we entwined our thighs. Metaphors and music, and otherwise a clean tongue on clean skin.

If I choose to think of someone else it's because I'll start crying and shaking as if she was with me now and we were together.

Most of all I'm like a willowtree in the wind.

Then the thought strikes me that we are two people, and that this is Hell.

He wants to go to the flicks, and I have no plans to go to the flicks. I'd rather fuck.

He would too, but suddenly, quite without a motive, he wants to keep abreast. He wants to import films. Go to Cannes.

I think: now I'll take a leap back to my innocence.

No one comes to find him.

His wife is on holiday. Always Mallorca, even though he's told her there are other places on this Earth worth visiting.

His daughter lives by herself now and never comes here.

He sits down on the Chinese (?) wicker chair, and rings, wet with sweat, to Gurli.

He would like her to be at home so they could meet for dinner. Like the old days. With candles, and red wine.

He takes a quick shower, stands in front of the mirror, in his dark trousers.

He does up the buttons of his white, newly ironed shirt. Ties his tie.

Then he sits down and puts on his shoes. They are shiny, black.

He takes a taxi into town.

They sit opposite each other at the little Italian restaurant.

She has this delightfully unimpressed attitude to life. At the same time glowing with gratitude over the wonders of existence. She loves her body.

He tells her about Italy. She enjoys hearing him talk, and smiles, and drinks the red wine.

He is walking along a beach. It is low tide. Late afternoon. The sand furrowed. Great lakes on the way out. The sun shines in the cloudless blue sky. The light on the water, reflections. It's turning.

She sits thinking of the clitoris and the G-point.

She has a weakness for older men.

They have style. And aren't so set on coming on.

He sits listening to Stravinsky.

They have a double Stock with the coffee. He loves spirits.

Then they'll go home to bed. They'll skip the flicks.

She lies on her stomach, legs spread. He undresses, slowly, watching her. Her breasts are pressed to the side. She's got a big bum. Lovely.

He has no problems with impotence. On the contrary. He has a mighty lust.

When she comes, she screams, so he nearly loses his breath.

She whimpers, and feels as if she has lost the whole world. He holds her.

He hovers above her, and sees her body shaking.

I sit, like warm air, on the high swing, with my beloved.

It's summer. Europe is full of nudes, but my beloved has chosen me.

He could have been anything. But I know very well what he is. He's just a bit of oblivion.

Together we'll forget everything.

A deep voice through the pillows. A roundabout where we sit on horses, penguins. It will go on, because I have him in my flesh.

The prick shoots out. I hook myself on, and my thighs tense. If I kneel, he will come from behind. I shut my eyes to see myself as a sex-opening.

Slowly, slowly, he comes further in. He is hard on me.

A sound, we slump down, with our hands out.

He's frightened.

He walks the streets like a hunted man.

He daren't go home.

He daren't walk the streets.

His clothes look quite wrong. He should be wearing jeans. Sweater. Desert boots. Sleeves pulled up over the elbows. And a windjacket over his shoulder. Teetering steps.

He walks quickly. Wrong. He's out of strength.

He sees the people. Their faces in the grey morning light. They smile while everything falls to pieces.

He's frightened.

There are so many identical animals in the dark.

He lies on a wet mattress that stinks of piss.

Outside all others, with their sorrows and roses.

He gets to his feet and finds his way to the light, grey daybreak in the tunnel of the street.

People come milling into one end, like a sea of insects. He is torn along with them, falls, gets up again and is drawn with the current down the street.

He goes from pub to pub. It's not his habit to drink so much beer.

Sitting on a bench, he thinks. But he does not succeed.

When I met him, he hadn't a sou on him.